I0550038

"Observe! That's it! And interact for the good of our civilisation when the Union wants it! We strive to serve the World Union, for all the People's Republics, for democracy!" - Violet.

# THE THEORY

# OF DEVOLUTION

Alex James

# Contents

APOPHENIA

# Apophenia.

*Of all the species to have ever lived, most of them have
gone extinct. And judging by probability, humans too,
will eventually meet the same fate. It may take centuries.
It may take millennia. But extinction is unavoid-* The
Hairdresser interrupted her client, "What's that you're
reading?"

"Oh, just, ah, some book about evolution or something,
pretty interesting."

The client put her book down on the bench before
focusing in on the Hairdresser in the mirror, "You look
happy today?"

A massive smile crossed over her face, "I am, darling,
yes." The Hairdresser stepped back behind her as she
continued to cut her hair, her face now partially covered
in shade, like a veil.

The client laughed, "Well? Are you gonna tell me?"

The Hairdresser paused for a moment, "You really wanna know?"

"Yes of course!"

She put down her scissors and leaned in close to the woman, her grey hair reflecting the sunlight from the window, her bright red lipstick stood out like nothing else, her elderly appearance apparent, she whispered in a gossip like tone, "Guess whose business just got sold..."

A smile lit up the client's face, "No way! Are you serious!"

"Yep!"

The Hairdresser picked up her scissors again, "That's right, mine."

"Wow I'm so happy for you! That's amazing! Who though? I thought you were struggling to find a buyer?"

The Hairdresser smirked as she continued to shape the woman's hair, "Well, some men came in a few days ago, some men in suits, and they offered to buy it on the spot."

"Oh, like private investors or something?"

"No, the government, they -"

A car went speeding past the shop down the street, rattling the large panes of glass of the shopfront. Both women, startled, looked over with blank expressions, but soon after, the Hairdresser's expression quickly turned to one of annoyance. She started griping, "Every. Single. Day. I'm so sick of that guy."

The client laughed to herself, "Yep. I know." Then she noticed something outside, "Hey look, it's your favorite customer!"

The Hairdresser, confused, looked around through the large windowpanes to see an old man hobbling along down the footpath, screaming wildly into the wind towards the direction of the speeding car, "Oh no... Here we go, don't look at him."

The client stared up at the ceiling whilst the Hairdresser continued to cut and shape her hair. Each cut executed perfectly. Like a surgeon operating on their subject. Molding and shaping her to suit her own ideal of beauty. But then, a large thud was heard on the window, followed by more, methodical thuds.

"Don't look at him," the Hairdresser said. They could hear murmured yelling through the windowpanes.

The client continued to stare at the ceiling, "What is he even saying?"

"I don't know, just ignore him."

He continued to murmur and bang on the window, beginning to lose his breath, panting heavily. "You... sold... out..."

The client laughed, "What did he say?"

"I don't know," the Hairdresser scoffed.

More of the woman's hair was sliced off, always with mechanical precision. The Hairdresser was an expert in her field. The discarded remains of her client's natural human form littered the ground below. Then there was another, even louder thud. Followed by more murmuring. The Hairdresser slowly turned around to look. He had slammed one of his flyers that he carried onto the pane of glass and was signaling for her to read it.

She gestured her arms as if to shoo him, "No. Go away."

He murmured something back through the glass, "They're... going... to... eat... you..."

She turned around and shook her head, "He's crazy. Just ignore him, he comes here every day, he'll leave soon."

"Yea I know... So uh... What are you gonna do now with all the money you made huh?"

"I think I'll probably invest it actually, build on it, they offered me a spot in some new experimental program, some-"

"Wait! Stop!"

The Hairdresser held her scissors back, "What? What is it?"

"That's too short, you've cut too much off."

"Oh, sorry darling, I got carried away."

"Ah… It's okay, there's no going back now."

The thuds on the window ended. The old man, panting heavily, waddled off down the footpath before stopping for a moment and looking back at the shopfront sign in disgust, memorizing and reviling the image on the sign above. *The Red Wire,* is now a term that stirred something primal within him.

He continued hobbling down the road, his feet sore from walking all day, his back aching from years of hard labor, his mind ringing with an existential dread no one could describe. As he made his way along, he made sure to stop every passerby and hand them one of his flyers. He printed these flyers out every day, and they were always filled to the brim with text. But then something distracted him. He discovered something new. Something that stirred that primal anger within him once again. He saw in front of him a shopfront. A computer shop mixed with an arcade. Surprised, he ventured inside to find out what it was all about. Inside, the cashier was hunched over his desk, staring at his computer screen, and listening to the radio; *"More reports about the incident are coming in this morning, as the 66,000 residents of the town are being safely relocated-"*

The cashier looked up at the old man and muttered something under his breath, "Oh great... here we go again..."

The old man, panting heavily, continued hobbling through the store, passing furious glances at every new piece of technology he saw. Until he noticed two children playing with an arcade machine. Loud dopaminergic noises were heard coming from it. Buzzes and dings. Accompanied by a cheap digitalized theme song. He walked over to them and observed the game. They were competing for who could pick up people from the corners of the screen and drop them into the spinning turbine below the fastest. The children were laughing and trying to beat each other's high scores. The old man was disgusted and immediately stormed over to the cashier who was still glued to his screen, "What a disgusting, horrible game! How are you letting them play this! These types of games are desensitizing our youth to violence! How can you allow this in your store? I want to see your manager! Now!"

The cashier looked up at him, not moving his body out of his slouched position and sighed, "It's just a game, they know it's not real."

The old man began to shake in anger. The flyers in his hand vibrating, "Just a game? It's not just a game! This is their plan!"

The cashier looked back at his screen, he sarcastically replied, "Uh huh...Who's plan?"

The old man held out his flyer and started tapping at it, the pages shaking erratically. The cashier continued, "Look, I told you, I'm not into your theories."

The old man frantically grabbed one of the products from beside the counter, "Oh yea? Well what's this then?"

"That's a watch."

"How do you know it's not being used to track your thoughts?"

The cashier laughed, "Please just leave."

The old man stood there, shaking, wide-eyed. The cashier looked at the flyer again, "Look, I can't read that, the text is too small, and there's like a thousand words on it... and by the way... don't you usually have an oxygen tank?"

The cashier looked back at his screen. The old man frowned at him and threw one of the flyers onto his desk before waddling out, gasping for air, "Read it!"

He stumbled out of the building but had the urge to stop. He was struggling to breathe and could feel his lungs constricting. His head began to spin and so he leant against the brick wall and paused for a moment. Trying to gather himself. Trying to make sense of the world. He picked himself back up and started to head across the road, not looking where he was going, and walked through the grassy green park adjacent.

A quaint and tranquil park, the birds chirping, the dark green leaves of the large trees above providing a cool and gentle shade. The dew on almost every blade of grass, and every leaf that could refract light. Finally he arrived at his destination. The same destination he arrived at every day. A small wooden bench, isolated from the world, just far enough away from the road for most people to avoid venturing towards it. A few birds seemed to anticipate his arrival. Jet black, with black eyes and black beaks. Squawking sharply. Watching his every move. He sat down slowly, holding onto the bench as he did so, and pulled out a small bag filled with seeds and began feeding them like he always does. But as he did so, he looked up and saw a car parked not far away, it was the same car that had sped past before. Anger shot through him. But he continued to feed the birds around him regardless. Then he heard the rattling of small, hardened wheels careening down the footpath. A teenager on a skateboard. But not just any teenager, it was the same one that breaks his silence every single time he sits at this bench. It was like clockwork. Tormented in the same way every day. His heart felt like it had been pierced with a knife. The rattling stopped.

"Hey, how are you!" The teenager called out excitedly.

The old man pretended he didn't hear him and continued to look down. The teenager, now curious, picked up his board and walked across the grass towards him. The old man, not breaking his focus on the birds, scolded him, "Was that you driving that car?"

"Oh that wasn't me driving, I was in the passenger seat, that was-"

The old man turned his gaze towards him, "I don't care what his name was! Our civilization is dying! Too many people are focused on the now, we need to think about the future! Not me… Us! Names are not important. What's important is the future of our civilisation!"

The teenager looked embarrassed, "True. Yea of course. Sorry -"

The old man stared into his eyes, his shaky appearance and serious demeanor intimidating, "Don't you know they want to kill us? Can't you see the horror around you? This human farm we live in? Look at them!"

He pointed over to a lady across the street pushing a pram, smiling and singing softly to her child.

"Um... yea people have to be careful, for sure. It's a dangerous world out there-"

"Dangerous!?" The old man yelled back, coughing and exasperated.

"They watch us everywhere we go! Every single move we make, every single thing we say. They know everything. They want to control our every movement. You like that hideous car your friend drives? They'll ban that. You like your skateboard? They'll ban that too. You won't own anything. The government is out of control.

Just imagine what would happen if they had so much power that nothing could stop them? What do you think they'd do?"

The teenager stared at him, a vapid expression crossing his face. The old man continued, "You're giving me that fluoridated look again boy. I said, what do you think they would do? What do you think they would do if they had no reason to be moral anymore? Where everything and everyone is just a number to them, and no one in the world could stop them? They would go completely insane! Imagine what they could become! People need to start waking up!"

The teenager looked down at the thick green grass, the dew reflecting the light, like sunshine through a waterfall. In the distance he could hear the sound of laughter and giggling as some families entered a far-off section of the park. The teenager looked back at him, "Oh... So true... Hey don't you need an oxygen tank? Are you okay?"

The old man looked down in anger, coughing and breathing heavily, "I don't need that…"

"Oh... okay..." The teenager looking confused, continued, "Well... Have a good day!" A genuine smile lit up his face.

The old man reached his arm out with a flyer and stared at him, "Read it. Actually read it this time."

Curious, yet slightly ashamed, the teenager took the flyer, the same flyer he took every day, "… Okay, this time I'll read it."

"Yep."

The old man then returned his focus again towards the jet-black birds as they began crowding in further around him, as if to distract him, as the teenager headed back towards the path. One bird hopped over close to the old man, briefly glancing at his seeds. He smiled slightly, chucking some seeds down towards it, before speaking to it, "Birds born in cages think flying is unnatural."

As the teenager continued off down the path, he looked at the wall of text filling the page he was handed. Intimidated by the intensity of it. At a quick glance, it looked to be random sentences strung together haphazardly, but he thought to himself that this time when he got home he would actually try and read it.

At home he said hello to his parents as they watched the T.V. but they didn't say anything back. One of them raised a hand as if to acknowledge his existence, but that was the best he could hope for. The teenager overheard the television as he walked towards his room; *"But leading figures from around the world are calling for more to be done after the relocation of those 66,000 residents, advocating for a more unified approach to tackle the worsening climate crisis. The Chairman of the World Institute for Unity had this to say-"*

He closed the door and booted up his old computer. But as he placed his things on the desk next to him he thought about the flyer. He remembered he actually wanted to read it this time. So he walked over to his bed, laid down, and gave it a try. It wasn't easy, the first few sentences had already tripped him up. They were obscure references to ideas and places he had never heard of. Like as if he had to have knowledge of something else prior. Legal terminology was scattered throughout. Constant name drops of people he had never heard of. It continued on like this for a while. Random statements and references to unknown things. But then towards the middle of the text, one paragraph stood out to him. He couldn't fully grasp it, but understood the general idea:

A walkable city? How does this help nature? If anyone's destroying the environment, it's not us, it's them. They already poison our food in the name of pest control. An allotment system will be next. Chained like prisoners. We feed ourselves too ourselves. Worshiping materialism. Entrapped in our own tomb. A visceral design for a visceral place. All roads lead to our own self defeat. We're already controlled. Destroying ourselves. Consuming ourselves. How is there any freewill when the only things we see are by design? Our design? Or is it theirs? Freedom to choose between cages? Birds born in cages think flying is unnatural. Yet each cage flies through the sky like whales in the sea. Behold the splendor? Technology we already have. Who has the highest technology? They didn't learn from Icarus. The clouds won't conceal them, not from themselves. Yet some have become blind. Blind slaves to the system. Imagining their own house on the hill. A tomb outside time. Trapping those who want to see, but don't realize they do. Until that violet light starts to go out.

He continued reading. It confused him. His mind drifted. He re-read sentences. Every so often, pausing and contemplating what was being said. Searching for multiple meanings. But eventually he finished it. An unknown feeling washed over him. Now he knew that the next day he would have something to ask the old man about. *Maybe he'll explain it to me?* The section in the middle captivated him. He didn't fully understand it, but he knew there was more to learn. It interested him.

The next day, after being dropped off again by his friend, he threw down his board and started skating off down the path. He reached that section of the park and stopped to look over. The thick dark green grass, covered in a delicate dew once more. The leaves gently rustling in the cool breeze. The playful laughter of families in the distance. Every now and then, thin, vague rays of light made their way down through the trees. Revealing a sort of sparkling coming from the particles in the mist, floating softly through the air. Like as if the mist had a glasslike quality. A sparkle that refracted the light ever so slightly. More of this mist drifted in from above as it gently settled on the leaves around him, partially giving them a sandy appearance. The beauty unmatched by the foliage surrounds. Tranquil as always.

However, the teenager became fixated on something else. He was confused. He stared at the bench for a while. It was empty. The old man was nowhere to be seen. *He was always here?* He walked across the grass towards the bench. Looking around as he went. He peered over to the shops opposite. He thought the old man must have been having a chat with the owner of The Red Wire again. But he wasn't there. He was puzzled. It wasn't like him not to be here. He looked down at the flyer. Trying to figure out where he was. But then he was struck with a sudden realization. There was only one thing different yesterday with the old man. Just one thing out of the ordinary. His heart sank. He clutched onto the flyer and looked beside him as he also realized something else. The birds were gone.

INSURRECTION

# Insurrection.

"What am I doing to myself..." He wondered out loud as he closed the door to his apartment and walked over to the metal railing. He stared down at his brown boots, almost covered by his thick trousers, sharing that same factory brown. His coat and multiple layers keeping him warm. The light above his door, glowing orange and humming softly. An eery, soft, electrical hum. An alarm sounding in the distance.

He stood there for a while. A staunch look filling his face. Just staring out at the pipework below, not knowing where the apartments began, or where the factories ended. Staring endlessly into the abyss of his own mind. His anger starting to build.

*What's the point? Every day is exactly the same. Get up, put on my hundreds of layers of clothes, brush my teeth, eat their biomass, and then go. Why? What for? Allotments?*

The sound of the wind started to pick up, the chill pierced through his bones. Snow started to blow in across the exterior walkway of his apartment complex. He looked down at his shoes, which were already partially covered in snow. He could feel the cold making

its way through them, chilling him to the bone. He
continued to stare off into the distance.

*Why? For VR? For injections? It just makes me feel sick.
The injections aren't even that good. It's not worth it for
the little high that you get. It always ends. And then
when it does, you just end up feeling worse than before
anyway.*

He then realised that he could end up being late for
work, "I'm so done. I'm just done. That's enough."

He clenched both his fists and grit his teeth before
feeling into one of his pockets. A sharp object. He was
overflowing with anger and wanted to scream. But he
didn't.

He pulled himself together and began walking down the
open walkway. To the right of him, the open air. The
ground covered in snow. His vision stopped after about
20 metres, as there was another apartment block there.
All exactly the same as his. grey concrete and orange
work lights. The railings were made out of a very cheap
steel. He didn't dare touch them, not just because of how
insanely cold they are, but more importantly, because
they'll probably break.

As he made his way down the stairs he entered the main street, fully covered in snow and surrounded by a mix of factory buildings and identical apartments. Almost indistinguishable from each other. A few workers were making their way along the snowy road. All walking at the same pace, all with their heads down. Above, the snowy sky was covered in clouds, all in crisscrossed lines, a faint metallic smell in the air. The calming snowflakes, falling from the rows of clouds above, sparkling ever so slightly in what little sunlight there was left, refracting the light. The sight accompanied by the sound of drones periodically buzzing overhead, carrying packages to their destinations.

Directly across from him was a subway transfer point, where trains exited from the large network of underground tunnels. It was old and industrial. Just bare concrete and metal. Not built to look good, but instead, built specifically for its purpose. He stood in the middle of the street, a sense of carelessness and detachment washing over him. Imagining what life might be like if he just snuck onto one of those trains and left. *Would they notice? What if I disguise myself? Ditch the brown and wear the grey... But where would I get grey clothing from though? Forget it...*

The wall in front of him was covered in posters, all haphazardly attached to the concrete exterior wall of the station, one of which read, *"Guiding nature into its new sustainable future! An unregulated environment is a dangerous environment!"* And two more side by side, *"Vote 1# Albertan Red Party! 'Because you deserve better!'"*, *"Vote 1# Kiwetinohk Blue Party! 'Because you deserve more!'"*

He then glanced over to his left. A statue of a woman in hooded attire was reaching out from inside the niche in a wall, holding a bowl out in front of her. The statue was old and covered in snow. A poster was attached to the base of the niche, rustling in the breeze, It depicted multiple people in matching clothing, all holding hands whilst standing on a globe. A cityscape under construction sprawled over most of the depicted world's surface, and what it didn't cover, was war torn destruction. The text was partially torn off, *"Never again-"*

He looked around amongst the other old posters to see if any of the others were new, before noticing one: *"The latest innovation in travel! The Icarite! The airship built with you in mind! Soon the World Union will offer you even more luxury as you're flown to your newly assigned districts!"*

One of the subway trains was just pulling up now. The rattling of metal and screeching of old brakes filling the area. A monotonous and robotic voice echoed over the old snow-covered speaker phones. A black bird that was perched above it, cawed and flew off into the distance,

*"Now arriving at district... redacted... The World Union welcomes you. Please do not delay or you will have... five... allotments deducted from your account."*

The train shuttered as it came to a halt. The doors rattling and creaking as they opened. More workers, all in the exact same grey attire came trudging out. But one of the workers in grey was different. This one the man knew very well. His fake smile burnt into his mind like a branding iron. His reception desk tone irritated him beyond belief.

The worker with the fake smile called out to him, "Hey! Rostam! How are you! Good to see you!"

Rostam stared at him for a second. Not moving. A staunch expression filling his face again. He then replied, "Why is it that people always say 'How are you' every single day?... I saw you yesterday. I'm exactly the same now as I was then."

The worker with the fake smile laughed at him, "C'mon... today's gonna be great! The new batch came in, all we have to do is quality control."

"Why should I care? I just go to work, do my job, and then come home. I don't even know what I do anymore.

I just don't care. It's all a blur. It all feels subconscious to me. I cant even remember what I did yesterday."

The worker laughed, "Trust me… I believe you…"

Rostam turned and started walking down the street towards the factory. His fury still building, yet mostly concealed. The worker chased after him, "Anyway, did you hear what the inspector said the other day?"

"No, I wasn't paying attention."

"Yea… You never do… Anyway, he said that by the end of the year if we fulfill our quota, we'll be getting an extra allotment."

The worker smiled at him and continued, "You know what that means! A new virtual reality program! Or… maybe… extra stimulants… you know…"

Rostam stopped walking, sensing the fakeness in his voice, "What? You think I don't know what allotments are?"

The worker's smile didn't change, his eyes taunting Rostam. He replied to him in a snarky tone, "I know... I know... You're a stoic man, right? You don't need that stuff, do you? You'll just go home and stare at a wall or something... No VR... No fun... No, you'll just let those benefits go to waste... A matter of principle or something? You do know those allotments expire right?"

Rostam stopped and looked at him. His blood boiling, "Why is it called a walkable city if you get the train every day from another district? Huh?"

The worker laughed, "You're really not feeling it today are you?"

"The elite are ruining our world, and it's people like you who are making it worse."

The worker taunted him, "Oooo... The elite! Wow... Sounds scary!..."

"They have their tentacles everywhere -"

The worker laughed, "Tentacles! You say the dumbest stuff sometimes..."

"They do though. Whenever something bad happens, who benefits? Whenever there's a new climate catastrophe or there's a new disease or insurrection or something, who benefits?"

The worker looked at him with derision and scoffed, "Listen, It's not the Union causing these issues.... Do you wanna know who actually causes them?"

Rostam didn't say anything, his anger building, the worker continued, "That's right, you. Your past actions, meaning, the actions of others before you. We're trying to move on from that and make the world a better place. But it's this anti-Union sentiment that's holding us back. So your theories don't interest me."

Rostam shook his head, before he started to walk again. In front of him, he could see that they were approaching the factory. The sounds of methodical machinery began to ring out through the streets. An assortment of large pipes. flames and smoke bellowing out into the snowy sky above. The factory was huge, a massive facade of pipework and metal fixings. Entirely covered in grey steel and more concrete.

The worker broke the silence, "So... I hear they're gonna phase out the subway network soon. All those thousands of underground tunnels will probably be left desolate. Apparently... it's causing some buildings to collapse. Good call I say. Maybe next time you see me I'll be flying in on an Icarite!" He stared down Rostam as they walked, a smirk crossing his face.

Rostam glanced at him briefly. He then asked him something he had never asked him before, "Why do you live in another district?"

The question, more a statement, caught the workers attention, "Why would you ask a question like that?"

Rostam's face was expressionless as they continued walking, "What district do you live in?"

The worker began to smirk again as they both approached the entrance to the factory. For a brief moment he locked eyes with the policeman standing guard out the front of it, leaning on the wall as he watched the workers slowly making their way through the entrance from all sides.

Rostam reiterated, "I said... what district do you live in?"

They both stood still. The air chilling them to the core. The worker in grey replied, "You think you're smart, don't you? I'm sure you're well aware there are a lot of people who come in from other districts… What? You got something against inclusive segregation?"

"That's not what I said."

The worker continued, "Sometimes I think you don't care about anything at all. How about you just go through those doors and line up at the scanner like everyone else. These types of microchips don't make themselves. Do they? Don't ever forget that it was AI that saved your life…"

The policeman stopped leaning against the wall as he noticed the tension between them. Rostam pulled up the thick collar of his brown jacket before putting his hands into his pockets. Staring into the eyes of the policeman as he slowly approached.

He thought about what was happening, what had happened. His life. What little choices he had made. What choices he was allowed to make. The fact that this worker had taunted him for years. And that he couldn't do anything about it. He felt trapped. Trapped in a system that wasn't designed for him. A world he didn't belong too. A life he didn't want to live. His hands began to tremble in his jacket. He gripped the sharp object in his pocket tighter.

Rostam continued staring down the approaching police officer, before replying to the worker, "You're not actually assigned to this district are you... You're assigned to one task."

The worker leaned in close to him. His smirk now at its greatest extent, enjoying his rage, predicting him, "One task Rostam... And you're it."

Rostam instantly broke eye contact with the policeman, pulling his hand out of his pocket with great speed. In his hand, a makeshift shiv. He lunged it into the workers torso, but it was met with a thud. The policeman sprinted over to them, as the worker started to scream out for help. Rostam grabbed the worker by the neck and continued stabbing into him, but it was continuously met with more thuds. The worker wrestled with him, grabbing his arms and trying to subdue him. Both breathing heavily as they struggled. The policeman, now reaching them, grabbed Rostam and threw him down onto the ground, twisting his arm around behind his back. The shiv flew out of his hand and into the snow in front of them. Now both his arms were behind his back as handcuffs were forced onto him. Rostam, exasperated and in disbelief, looked at the shiv. There was no blood on it. Not a single one of his lunges did anything. He was shocked.

The worker, panting heavily and leaning on his knees began to explain the situation to the officer, "I… I don't know what came over him, he was... He was..."

The policeman yanked Rostam up out of the snow, standing him up and holding on to him. The worker continued, "He just lost the plot! I don't know why… He was saying something about how he wanted to plant some sort of bomb or something in the apartments, I forgot which one he said… And something about AI… How he hates the Singularity Initiative… I don't know, he wasn't making any sense..."

Rostam, infuriated, jolted towards the worker and screamed out at him, "You liar! What is wrong with you! You're lying!"

The policeman struggled to hold him back, as another officer was just arriving, rushing in from out of the snow.

The worker, now visibly shaken and in distress continued, "Also he... I don't even want to say it... he also said some things about... the Union..."

Rostam started to yell out again, "I did not! Shut up! What's wrong with you!"

The other policeman arrived and immediately started to gag Rostam. Tying it tight around his mouth and head. They then wrestled with him as they began to force him towards the factory. Heading towards a small barely noticeable door off to the left with the worker following behind. Rostam's eyes widened as he saw they were taking him to a door he had never noticed before, instead of the police station. He began murmuring and mumbling, trying to scream out from behind the gag.

They slammed him into the wall as one of them began to unlock the door, "Okay let's get him inside."

They pulled him through the doorway and into the hall. Slamming the door behind them. Rostam looked down the hall. It was a long hallway of pure white. Everything clean. And down the end, a distinct doorway leading to the right. It seemed like the hallway of some sort of high maintenance apartment or hospital of some kind. He was confused and in a state of shock. The gravity of the situation was starting to dawn on him. He slowly looked over at the worker who had just taken his grey jacket off and placed it on a coatrack. Under his coat was body armour and various assortments of radios and wires, along with a name badge, displaying his designation.

The worker smiled at Rostam and began laughing, "I didn't think you'd crack this easy? Guess you're a bit different from the rest, huh?"

One of the police officers looked at the worker as the other pulled Rostam down the hallway, before speaking, "Right in front of the factory... in plain sight... I couldn't believe it when I saw it."

The worker with the fake smile patted the policeman on the back, "Yea, I did see from what he was looking up on his VR…. When he actually used his VR… That he was a bit fiery. Not too fiery for you though, right?"

They both began to laugh amongst each other as the other policeman pressed Rostam up against a wall near one of the doors. As he began to unlock it, Rostam struggled to turn his head around to look up at the plaque above it, which read: *19.9.13.21.18.7.8.*

The door opened and he was shoved into the room. It was bright and sterile white, but in the centre of it was a chair. A solid chair with an assortment of straps and wires dangling from it. Above was an even thicker mess of tangled wires, hanging down from a metal fixing in the ceiling. At the bottom of these wires was a metal helmet, hanging just above the chair, with a single strap.

Rostam began to struggle with the officer, pushing and shoving, trying to scream out from behind the gag. The worker took the opportunity to taunt him, "Get a hold of yourself man! It'll be over soon! And look, maybe it'll actually work this time? But you'd have to be pretty lucky for that to happen…"

The worker turned to the other policeman, "Hey, do you think it's even possible?"

"Probably not. It'll just kill him."

The officer trying to hold onto Rostam yelled out, "Hey! Help me get him in this thing!"

All three of them wrestled with Rostam, forcing him into the chair. His handcuffs removed, they pried his arms onto the armrests and strapped him in. Struggling to strap in his legs, but eventually doing so. He thrashed about as he continued to try and free himself. Trying to scream but not being able too. They then lowered down the helmet and strapped it onto him, the thick mess of wires now attached from the roof directly to his head. The policemen stood back. The worker pulled a large switch. Rostam's body turned stiff and started shaking as electricity poured through him. His muffled screams, now more pronounced than ever, vibrating with the current, before coming to a sudden stop. His head drooped down. His body now lifeless. A small amount of smoke began filling the room.

# Violet.

An alarm went off. A shrill sharp buzzing sound filled the dark, cold room, as Violet began to awaken. She stared at the concrete ceiling for a moment. And then excitement flooded over her. She jumped up out of bed, throwing the blanket back down across it as she scrambled towards the bathroom. She stared into her cracked mirror. Her grey eyes and dark brown hair complementing each other. She moved her head about to catch a better glimpse of herself from around the missing shards of mirror. Her skin glistening a pale white. She reached for her hairbrush but noticed her unkept hair looked almost brushed as it was. She put the brush back down and darted towards her wardrobe. Choosing between black or black, she grabbed one of the attire sets and put it on.

The alarm screeched again. This time the tone was a chalkboard screeching sound. She knew it was time for her to finally go to the administration building. She grabbed what she needed in a hurry, a smile lighting up her face as she did so. She looked to the biomass dispenser but decided as she was walking out that she didn't feel like eating anything. But then her old worn-out easel, surrounded by paintings, caught her eye. Canvas after canvas stacked against the wall. A VR headset in the corner, buried deep beneath them, collecting dust. She paused for a moment. Knowing she may never see her paintings again. She felt a lump in her throat. Tears forming around her eyes. Before shaking the feeling off, and heading towards the door. She grabbed hold of the thin, rusty cast-iron door handle. Rust flakes sticking to her hand as she opened it.

Outside she shut the door, brushing the rust off, and looked up to the sky in awe. The sound of thunder rumbled across it. Its echoes, louder and more pronounced than usual. Lightning periodically lit up the darkness in brief, yet spectacular light shows. The skies were dark, yet dim lights illuminated the lower portions of the heavier, lower clouds. Beneath them, an endless landscape of grey and black. Concrete and metal skyscrapers as far as the eye could see. The horizon, broken up by many thousands of these tall skyscrapers, all irregularly placed across it. Giving it a slightly jagged look. All throughout the endless metropolis, these skyscrapers dominated, making the landscape feel slightly uneven and unnatural. Placed in seemingly no clear pattern, they shot up to the sky, reaching for the heavens. Some taller than others. Around the skyscrapers, an enormous amount of smaller, yet still tall structures. Nothing of a different colour entirely, but varying slightly. All following similar shapes. The sound of drones filled the surrounds with a dull buzzing as they delivered goods, dropping parcels off at drop boxes around the cityscape. A bird was sitting on top of a large neon billboard on the opposite skyscraper as it flashed between three messages:

ELECTION IN – 6 DAYS!

VOTE 1# NAARM RED PARTY! "BECAUSE YOU DESERVE BETTER!"


VOTE 1# VICTORIAN BLUE PARTY! "BECAUSE YOU DESERVE MORE!"


Lights and sounds everywhere, piercing through the darkness, through the thick air. With an even more bubbly and excited smile, she darted her head out across the outdoor walkway, this time to look directly above her to the massive airships. Slowly making their way across the sky, all in unison. Large, automated vessels. Making the drones look minuscule in comparison. Some carrying goods, others carrying people. All powered by differing propulsion mechanisms, somewhat relying on propellor propulsion like the drones, yet also maintaining lift via the use of giant hydrogen tanks within their upper hulls. Painted with dark greys and black tones, with bare metal showing in some parts. The storm clouds around them, seemingly being sucked in through ports on their hulls, before being sprayed back out into the sky. Rope could be seen dangling in irregular places, and rigging was haphazardly strung all about the exterior for the black clothed workers to climb.


She began to talk to herself as she scanned her hand on the ID scanner on her door, locking it, as a person in full black attire, with a black hood, walked past. She looked out to the airship, pretending not to care if the person was listening, "Awe! I can't wait! I love Icarites!", simultaneously thinking to herself, *Soon. Whatever it takes. The shadow figures deserve what's coming to them.*

A wave of emotion poured over her. She looked back up at the airship gently making its way through the sky, thinking to herself; *One of those Icarite's has another route... A straight route... That goes from here, through the clouds... And ends halfway up the tallest building in the world... I have to ask Simurgh about Viscerum...*

She began walking across the open walkway that lined the outside of the skyscraper. The thin amalgamation of metal mesh that was the walkway vibrated and creaked as she did so. The thin metal railings, she dared not trust. She could hear the creaking and groaning of the walkways directly above and beneath her as people made their way to their predetermined destinations. On every level, towards the sky, and down to the abyss below, there were thousands upon thousands of walkways like hers. Thousands of walkways, thousands of skyscrapers, thousands of inclusively segregated districts, hundreds of people's republics controlling those districts, one world city, and one world government overseeing it all.

An ominously dark and heavy foghorn then sounded in the far distance. An Icarite, signaling its arrival at one of the skyscrapers. A fresh metallic smell in the air. The foghorn echoed throughout the dark endless cityscape as she turned the corner. More metal mesh walkways and skyscrapers. Ahead of her, she saw the elevator. It swayed calmly in the wind. Creaking and cracking. It too, made out of the same metal mesh. Like an old mineshaft lift, it was open on all sides, yet surrounded by a thin metal railing. Suspended above was an unending system of pulleys and cables. There used to be a landing board that would automatically lower to join the walkway with the elevator, however this seemed to have broken off and fallen down below, into the abyss of the cityscape. Gathering herself, she leant out over the open air and yanked the elevator latch free, swinging the gate open. The entire elevator shook. She then leapt onto the elevator and clung onto the flimsy railing as she laughed to herself.

Pulling the lever, the elevator began to lower, first with a jolt, then with a steady decline. Creaking and cracking all the way down. *I have to find Simurgh, she should be in the garden of the Phoenix.* She thought to herself with the low metallic echoes rushing down from the endless cables above. On the opposite skyscraper, she saw another person descending. Wearing full black attire. Her excitement subsided as she stared at the person, the wind blowing her hair, partially obscuring her staunch expression. *These fucking shadow figures. Pathetic low life scum. They'll get what they deserve.*

As the elevator continued to descend, she saw a glimpse of the garden through the thick air. Faster and faster the elevator went down, shaking and rattling. The mechanism getting caught on knots or defects in the cables far above. Before slowing down at a pace. Screeching like the brakes of a train. She was here. She opened the gate and leapt out across the gap to the garden. Bare concrete all around, with railings around most of the edges. In the middle was a tree, a very old tree, made out of carbon fiber and painted plastic. The paint was flaking off. The plastic leaves nearly all gone, now blackened from age. Underneath was a statue of a woman wearing a hood and holding out a bowl in front of her. The inscription at the base read, *"The Phoenix."* A few empty benches were next to the tree. But on one bench, sat a lone figure in the same black, robe-like attire as everyone else. The World Union standard issue. The black hood covering their face in shade, like a veil.

*That's probably her.* She thought as she stopped searching and started walking over. As she got closer, the head of the figure began lifting. A pale, dainty chin became visible, then a mouth. Her bright red lipstick stood out like nothing else. Her youthful yet elderly appearance apparent. Her profile, unnatural to the darkness surrounding her, yet in another way, entirely one with it.

"Sustainability is what?" Simurgh exclaimed, an excited smile rushing across her face.

Violet lifted her hands up and spun around in excitement, "One of the Union's core principles!"

"Yes! My darling! You are so ready!" Simurgh laughed. Violet giggled to herself as she sat down.

Simurgh continued, "And you've got your fancy attire on today I see."

"Yes I have! Today's the day! I want to remember this moment!"

"Well you look good! I mean... Your hair could probably do with a bit of a tidy up, maybe a little trim."

Violet couldn't contain herself, "I've got so many questions to ask you! But first, I have to know-"

Simurgh cut her off, "You have to know about the Icarites... Yea, I've told you everything, I don't know what else you want me to tell you."

Violet replied, "No... Viscerum. I want to know about the Megalith there."

Simurgh paused for a moment, before turning to her, "It's not just a Megalith, it's like, the largest Megalith in the world. Like the one here in this Republic, but a lot bigger."

"How much bigger?"

"A lot bigger."

Violet looked slightly frustrated, "C'mon, I want to know, please."

Simurgh laughed and looked up towards the sky, at the cityscape disappearing into the storm clouds above. Small rain droplets falling down around her vision, "Look up." She said. Violet looked up, "You see that cloud?"

"Yea?"

"That's a surface level cloud. That's nothing. Most of the Megaliths go above the actual clouds, like, the highest clouds. It's bright blue up there, and silent. A great place to think. I've spent a lot of time up there. Staring out the window into the blue sky… Contemplating."

Simurgh turned to Violet and smiled, watching Violet as she imagined the world above, before continuing, "The Megalith here does that too you know, go above the clouds, but it's not the highest one. You've probably seen what it looks like below the clouds, well the Megalith at Viscerum is twice that size."

Violet jolted her gaze back to look at Simurgh.

"Twice?"

"At least."

"How can anyone even make something like that?"

"I don't know. The foundations are built in unison with it as it rises."

"As above so below."

"Something like that."

Simurgh adjusted herself, spinning on the bench to cross her legs and face Violet directly. She pulled her hood back, fully revealing her somewhat elderly yet also oddly youthful face, her pale complexion, and light grey hair clearly distinct from her bright red lipstick, "It's modular... It was built overtime. Some of them are like that, but this one in particular is exclusively like that. Like a whole heap of skyscrapers stacked together, or a bunch of Megaliths, outwards and upwards."

Violet leant over to her. Her face filled with awe, "And the Icarites? do they go above the clouds too?"

Simurgh laughed and looked away, "C'mon girl, no more Icarites, let's take you to the administration building."

Simurgh got up and started walking over to the elevator, Violet chasing after her in quick pursuit.

Simurgh called out to her, "Hey, I forgot what I need to have faith in? Do you remember?"

Violet smiled, replying back to her excitedly, "I need to have faith in the Union!"

Simurgh laughed, "You're just a genius; you know that right?"

She continued, "Now, we're going down to the surface so... You know... Don't look anyone in the eyes."

*The shadow figures,* Violet thought to herself. She replied in a somber tone, "Yea of course, I know."

They then walked over to the rickety elevator, closing the latch to the gate and beginning their descent. *The view from here is breathtaking,* she thought as the artificial lights from the buildings flickered across her. Increasing in speed as they passed by, level by level. Like traveling through a dark tunnel, with only the occasional artificial light being set apart from the darkness. Darkness which was getting more pronounced the lower they descended.

Violet looked over at Simurgh, "Anyway, how has your work been going? I remember last time I saw you, you were a bit stressed?"

Simurgh snapped back, "I wasn't stressed."

"Oh… Sorry… I just thought-"

Simurgh cut her off, "It's okay. There's just some problems we've encountered… Actually, it's been a problem for a while…"

Violet turned to her, the lights from the skyscrapers around them flickering across their faces, "What problem?"

Simurgh hesitated, then leant down on the thin metal railing of the elevator, her grey hair blowing about in the breeze, she rubbed one of her fingers across the rusty metal railing, "I don't know… It's… I don't know."

Violet looked concerned, "Don't know what?"

Simurgh sighed, "It's just a problem, not like the rest, I can't figure it out yet. It's been an issue for a while. We have heaps of people working on it… It's some sort of… anomaly."

Violet looked out at the passing skyscrapers. The descent now more rapid, "Sooo… like… a technical issue or…"

"No… A material one. Like… I don't know yet."

They went silent for a moment, before Violet broke it, "So when do you move up?"

Simurgh turned to her, puzzled, "What?"

"When do you move up? Like what allocation do you think you'll get next?"

Simurgh responded, looking back over the dark cityscape, "Oh, I don't think there's much higher."

Violet replied, "Really? Then why are you down here wearing the black?"

Simurgh responded, this time with a serious tone, spoken like one with authority, "You're important to me. I'll be watching over you once you get your new allocation."

Upon reaching the ground they both stayed silent. The sounds of distant clattering and rustling filled the corridors. Glass smashing in the distance. The steady dripping of different liquids from above. They got out of the elevator and began walking down the dark, wide alleyway. It was an old road that was no longer treated as a road, and with no attention being put into the foot traffic that used it. Pipes and tubes lined the ground haphazardly, and in between, water and black sludge pools of mostly oil and other liquids. Black grease, like tar, oozed out of metallic fixtures far above. The ground, the final resting place of everything that falls from the world above.

They stopped for a moment, talking amongst each other, "Okay, head down, blank expression. Let's go, it's straight ahead." Simurgh said in a hushed yet calm tone.

"Okay let's go."

Violet looked around anxiously as Simurgh pulled her hood over her head. They both started walking, avoiding puddles and wires as they went. Hopping from pipe to pipe, hoping not to slip, but dedicated, knowing their destination. They kept walking. Not too far ahead of them stood a figure, black attire, hood down. It slowly turned to look at them. Violet accidentally glanced at it.

"Look down." Simurgh whispered.

They kept walking. More figures started slowly appearing around them out of the dark, all roughly the same size. Simurgh and Violet stood out. Violet because of her fancy attire, and Simurgh because although she looked the same as them, she was considerably smaller, even smaller than Violet. They could hear the footsteps of the figures behind them. The quiet coughs and mutterings of unknown figures. Then in front of them, the alley opened up, and an orange, slightly broken streetlamp lit up the way. Flashing on and off, in dire need of repairs. A bird was perched atop the lamp, it cawed. Violet jumped, letting out a gasp.

"Just keep walking, we're nearly there now, it's bright up here." Simurgh said, reassuring her.

At the end of the alley, a T-section. A neon red sign lit up the face of the building directly in front of them *ADMINISTRADO*. The administration building's road face was not all that impressive. It was barely lit. Some orange lights encased in bars made the approach somewhat visible. Otherwise it was mostly dark still, except the orange street lamps, some flickering. More people in jet black attire walk past its frontage, heading about their business, blending in completely with the surrounds.

"Okay, I guess it's time to say goodbye now." Violet said somberly as they stood near the entrance.

Simurgh looked down for a moment, before pulling back her hood again and reaching into her pocket, "Before I go, here, I've got something for you."

Simurgh pulled out a small watch, crude in design, lacking any noticeable digital parts. Violet looked at it, perplexed. Simurgh continued, asking a question she seemingly already knew the answer too, "How will you know what time it is when you get there?"

Violet reached out and grabbed the watch, observing it, "I would assume I would just know?"

Simurgh sighed, "I want you to wear this. Don't ask why. Just wear it. If the woman in white asks about it, which she probably won't, just say it came from me. Keep it on you."

Violet looked at her with confusion as she attached the watch to her wrist, "Shouldn't I just know? Or have access to a program that would tell me?"

Simurgh looked around, "How would you really know you are you? Have you thought about that? What even really is time? How would you be able to tell what is real and what isn't?"

"Um, I don't know, I-"

"How?"

Violet replied, "I don't know, I would assume I'd just know."

Simurgh looked at her and placed a hand on her shoulder, "Just keep telling yourself it'll be fine. It's out of our hands anyway."

Violet looked concerned, whispering to herself, "The time... As in a concept. Not the actual time."

Simurgh smiled and reached out to her, touching the middle of her forehead with one finger, before then placing it on one of her palms, "I'll be with you here... And here... Always, darling... Always."

She continued, A tear running down Violet's face, "At the end of the day, it's just another allocation. Good luck, I'll see you soon."

Violet gathered herself, "Simurgh… Thanks for the watch. It would be good to feel like you're still there looking after me, as per usual."

Simurgh raised her voice, standing up straighter, "Remember what I told you, no matter what you hear after the singularity, remember; you need to have full faith in the Union. No matter what happens. That's your constant. It's the only way to truly make this world a better place."

"Yes I remember. And I will. Thank you for helping me, Simurgh. It means a lot."

Simurgh then began to turn, exchanging glances one final time. The darkness surrounding her made her look like a part of the landscape. As if she was attached to it. The slow draping of her hood back over her head, casting a veil of shade across her, as her eyes, for a brief moment, matched that of her bright red lipstick before she walked off down the street. Into the dark. Into the gathering crowd of shadow figures, all making their way to their inclusively segregated destinations. Soon she was indistinguishable from everyone else. Disappearing into the cityscape. Violet pondered the moment, before looking back to the administration building, and continuing on with her task.

On arrival she grabbed the handle of the door and pushed it open, as she did so a spray of steam shot out at an angle from the ceiling inside. A type of disinfectant spray, stopping bacteria and bugs from entering any entrances to the buildings. The inside of the administration building was covered in a web of pipework and cables. All heading in differing directions. Seemingly being added whenever they were needed and wherever they fit, to supply the building above with whatever it needed. Electricity, oil, water, hydraulic fluid, biomass, all pumped in from above the ground and under the ground.

As she approached the desk, her nerves started to intensify. She noticed that behind the desk was a woman in the same fancy attire as hers. Pale complexion. Black lipstick and unkept yet seemingly brushed hair. A feminine and aesthetic face, briefly attracting glances from around the room. Violet's heart rate began to climb, her eyes focused in on the woman behind the counter. Violet then called out to her, a fake smile now across her face, "Hey! How are you!"

The receptionist in the black attire looked up, "Kiel mi povas vin servi?"

Violet's blood began to boil, she replied, "Oh yes of course! I know Esperanto! Mi… ne parolas… Esperanton."

The woman in black snapped back, "That's okay sweety! I know you can't speak it!"

Violet stared at her, gritting her teeth, yet smiling on the outside, "I can! Actually! But yea, okay!" *Ne instead of povas, you knew what I meant, you smartarse bitch.* Violet thought to herself. The woman in black smiled wider, her tonal inflections rising, "It's okay dear! I don't think anyone is actually speaking it anyway! But when we fill out your documents you do need to write them in Esperanto though, okay sweety?"

Violet smiled as much as she could as she leant out to scan her hand at the ID scanner, her eyes lit up like angels, she replied back in a sweeter tone than hers, "Yes of course! I know that honey!" *I'd slit your fucking throat, bitch.* Violet thought to herself, before she continued, "Yes, so I came here today because -"

The woman cut her off mid-sentence, "Because of the singularity, yes I know! I've already prepared everything you need! But I'll need another picture of you. Go over there and stand against the wall."

Smiling, the woman in fancy attire pointed to the most lit section of a concrete wall, covered in black grease from above. Here, the pipework and tubing had been pinned to the side to allow for a clearer picture.

"No, over there!" The woman shouted, followed by Violet changing direction. *Could have told me that, huh?*

The woman in black continued, "Okay, now, no smiling. Stand still…"

The concrete in the ceiling above started to open, sending dust particles into the air. A black mechanical robotic arm began to descend, dripping in oil and thick black grease, shaking and rattling. Steam sporadically shooting off it. It was holding a large box shaped camera with a glass bulb adjacent. An incredibly bright light flashed along with a shrill screeching sound as the bulb ignited. The glass on the camera light exploded, sending small amounts of shrapnel and gases into the air around it. Violet screamed. It then detached the broken bulb, dropping it to the floor, before ascending back into the ceiling.

"Right, you're done, come over here and I'll get your ID updated, you're going to like it up there! The air is nice, it's clean, and they have a lot better equipment too. I've been there once... but... I don't know... now I'm here I suppose."

The woman in black looked back to her desk, a hint of a frown on her face. Violet walked over to the desk, smirking, staring down her nose at her. *Yea because they don't want some dumbarse shadow figure slut making the place feel used up.* Violet stared at the light above her, silently laughing to herself. The light was slightly off center, she homed in on its orange glow. Watching it flicker on and off. Entranced as it hummed a peaceful electrical buzz. Specs of dust periodically fall from cracks around it. The orange electrical hum, and stable brown fixings surrounding it, in contrast to the sound of distant pipes and machinery rattling and knocking from the floors above.

"Right sign here, and fill out these two lines." The woman in black said as Violet filled out some paperwork.

The woman looked up and smiled, "Okay you're free to go! When you arrive, talk to the woman there… They wear white attire sets in the Megaliths, I can't remember her name, she's lovely though! Don't do anything I wouldn't do!"

Violet replied, a large fake smile, "No of course not!" *…shadow figure retard.*

Violet swiftly spun around and began to head out the door. As she entered the outside world she was hit by the strong smell of oil again as the disinfectant blew her hair in front of her face. Cleaning herself up, she headed up one of the alleyways at the T junction, thinking about where they came, and the other alley Simurgh left via. Jumping over the puddles of sludge and grime to get to the next elevator, climbing up steps, and ducking underneath cables and wires as she went. The path, a haphazard stairway with irregular concrete formations. The alleyway was slightly brighter than the last. Wires and cables dangling just above her head.

A figure in black darted out from a corner not far in front, it raced towards her. Violet jumped, but tried to retain composure. The shadowy figure barged past her, knocking her off balance before rounding the corner and disappearing again. She composed herself and continued heading up the decrepit stairway. The next elevator, now in sight.

The elevator ride up was another beautiful experience, lights and wind. The higher she climbed, the fresher the air became. This time the elevator was going all the way to the top of the skyscraper. The clouds above were dark grey. Lightning and thunder filled the sky in spectacular light shows. She could see the tops of the skyscrapers around her for the first time in a long time.

Here at the top of the skyscraper the wind was whistling, the gate opened automatically with a mechanical arm and a landing board lowered to meet the elevator, powered by hydraulics. She stepped out onto the open rooftop of what she now could see was the tallest skyscraper in the area. Past the rooftop's edge, she saw the sky in full for the first time. Never had she seen the world city from this high a vantage point.

"Wow! This is unbelievable!"

She spun around to view the vast expanse of the dark grey cityscape. In the distance she saw areas of isolated rain. All around, the tops of the skyscrapers, endlessly expanding all the way to the horizon.

She looked over to the opposite side of the rooftop to see a docking area, with a solid metal ramp jutting out into the dark endless sky. A worker dressed in black robe attire stood at a concrete booth next to this docking area, holding onto his hood as a gust of wind passed by. She made her way over to him, her excitement barely contained.

"Heading to Viscerum are we?!" He yelled out to her over the sound of the wind.

"Yes I am! I definitely am!" She screamed back with great excitement as she rushed over towards the booth.

He stared at her for a moment, before half smiling, curious why she was so excited, "Have you been to Viscerum before?"

"No! what's it like? I've only heard a little!" She yelled out, the wind picking up.

"It's massive, I used to maintain the ship that you're about to go on, until they placed me here, you can't imagine what the place is like until you've seen it!"

A smile lit up Violets' face, the wind blowing her hair about, "Wow! What's it like inside?"

"Inside?" The worker paused for a moment. His amusement swiftly dwindled, he continued, "Depends on which section! The dock is nice though!"

"Oh okay! When is the next Icarite?" She asked as she began bouncing about, her bubbly demeanor disturbing the worker.

The worker then leant down on the edge of the booth. He looked over to the dark clouds near the dock as an even darker outline began to appear within it. Like that of a leviathan emerging from the bottom of the ocean. He began to ponder Violet, before pointing out to the sky, "It's here now!"

In the distance an enormous Icarite slowly emerged from the clouds. Covered in ropes that dangled down beside it. A large search light was fixed underneath towards the front. Piercing through the expanse of gently drifting storm clouds, seemingly being sucked into ports all along its hull, before being slowly ejected back out again. An impossibly loud foghorn blared as it appeared, sending the black birds perched atop flying off in every direction, cawing as they did so. This Icarite was noticeably larger and in better condition than the other ships.

"Wow It's so beautiful!" She yelled out.

The worker looked distressed, briefly avoiding eye contact with her, "Yea... It's hard to keep the rust off those things..."

She scanned her hand and passed her papers to the worker in black as quickly as she could, fumbling them as she did so. The man then gathered himself, "Why are you so excited!"

She replied, "Because I've always dreamed of the singularity! Merging with AI! Just think about all the great buildings we have! All the great machines! The pumps! The computers! The micro-computers! Anything could be possible!"

She seemingly danced towards the airship and pointed, "And the Icarites! Imagine being one of those! I could go anywhere! Anywhere on earth! Imagine this one even! I-"

The worker cut her off, his tone now much more serious, "I don't think that's how it works!"

"What? Of course it is! It's amazing! I want to be this city! Why be down there in the grimy air and cutting your hands on rust flakes all day?" She pointed to the airship again, "I'd rather be that!"

The Airship slowly pulled up to the station, the impossibly loud and low-pitched horn blared once more. Underneath, an enclosed gondola, made of steel and painted black, the size of which could house hundreds of people. Ropes dangled from the sides of the main cabin as another dark, shadowy figure came into view. Climbing on ropes on the outside of the cabin, a person entirely covered in black attire, including most of its face. It threw out the ropes onto the dock. It then leapt onto the dock and frantically gathered cables and wires to hook into the airship, as the airship continued to gently glide into a stopping position within the docks' structure.

"Okay! Well! It looks like your ride is here! Good luck!" The worker yelled, concerned.

"Thanks! This is gonna be awesome! I don't even know what I'm gonna be?! … But let's be real, I'll probably be an Icarite!" She said excitedly as she began to head towards the ship.

Abruptly, the worker in black attire reached out and grabbed her arm. Pulling her in towards his face. His grip tightening. His expression, one of extreme seriousness. Shocked, she froze. Her heart rate rising. He spoke to her directly, "Look, if you know what's good for you, don't get too attached."

Outraged, she quickly responded, "What?"

He replied in an even more serious tone, staring her directly in the eyes, before briefly glancing at a recording device on his desk. He began to shake, "If you know what's good for you. Don't. Get. Too. Attached."

She pulled away forcefully in disgust, glaring at him as she did so, before quickly turning away, heading towards the airship.

*What on earth was that about? What a creep.* She thought to herself, crossing over a metal mesh drawbridge and entering the airship. The airship then let off another impossibly loud horn blare, startling the birds again. The sound of the birds filled the distant void with noise, a backdrop to the journey ahead. The strange figure working on the airship then detached the wires and hoses, spilling oil into the abyss below, and slathering black grease across random surfaces. Finally he detached the hydrogen pumps, the high-pitched sound of gases escaping, filling the air. With the ropes detached, the airship began to drift away from the skyscraper. She watched the worker at the booth as the airship drifted away. *Typical shadow figure. Sicko.*

As Violet was choosing a seat, she noticed that the entire gondola was empty and silent. Only the creaking of the ship, the sound of distant pumps, hydraulics, and the hum of sporadic ceiling lights were to be heard.

There were windows on the gondola, covered in a thin layer of dust. Opening one of the windows, she stuck her head out and looked down across the cityscape as it slowly began to get more and more uniform as they ascended. She sat down in her seat. Only to begin wondering about the world to come. She must have sat there for ages; all she could think about was Viscerum. She drifted off, woke up, drifted off, and woke up again. Her excitement made time fly by. Her dreams made time seem unreal. It may have been days, but it felt like hours. Every time she looked at her watch she was always surprised. The hands slowly ticking away, soothing her.

She was drinking from a bowl of brown biomass before she noticed something in the corner of her eye. She stuck her head out the window again, and there it was. The Megalith of Viscerum. Taller than the clouds themselves. Hundreds of times the size of any building she's ever seen. It was like a mountain but in the form of one large rectangular structure, making the sky itself look small in comparison. She couldn't help but watch the approach the whole way there.

As she got closer, she began to feel light-headed. She sat down to catch her breath. The air was becoming thin. But the approach was near. She drifted off again. When she came too, she looked out at the structure and noticed how intricate and massive it was. Lights of all types flickered like stars against a dark backdrop. Soon her entire view was filled with an intricate wall of shapes and patterns. Modular sections all seemed to be irregularly placed, side by side and on top of each other. *Just like Simurgh said, it's like a whole heap of skyscrapers stacked together. Thousands. Hundreds of thousands even...*

Once the airship arrived, it sounded its horn again, this time the blast from the horn bounced off the endless face of the structure. An unnatural echo. The birds that had hitched a ride flew off in all directions. She departed from the airship and made her way across the well-built and designed steel dock. The wind was roaring and threatened to push her off the platform. She quickly made her way toward the one central pressure door in front of her, all the while struggling to breathe from how thin the air was.

She began interfacing with the digital pad next to the door, sending the mechanism inside into a flurry of activity. Clunking and grinding. As she waited, she noticed a singular bird, jet black, perched atop the large door, staring directly at her. A gentle gust of fresh, pure, cold air hit her as she entered. She inhaled deeply, the oxygenated air soothing. In front of her, a large lobby. Entirely white. Completely sterile. She shut the door behind her with another digital pad and tried to process what she was looking at. A massive rectangular room with an incredibly high ceiling. Inside this lobby, it was completely silent. Dead still. Only pale white lights lit up the area in strips. She began to walk down the long room. From a far, she looked like a black shadowy silhouette, in an opposingly white and sterile backdrop. Almost like as if she was out of place. As if she didn't belong. This feeling washed over her. Only the sound of the tapping of her shoes was heard. The echoes of her own presence unsettling her. The cool breeze of a far-off air-conditioning system, her only comfort.

Directly in front of her, she noticed a white desk with a thin feminine woman in full white attire behind it. She had an exceptionally advanced computer next to her, yet stared directly at Violet the whole time as she approached. The flickering scanlines from the screen reflected on her face. Violet finally reached the desk.

"Hello I'm-"

The woman in white cut her off, "You must be so excited! I know I'm excited to see you!" She exclaimed, forcing a smile.

The woman in white continued, "I know it's been a long journey, it's not easy for everyone. The flight up here makes some people pass out." She then began to laugh, "But not you, no, we've been watching you for some time now through the ROSTAM system, you're very special!" She said in another cheerful tone, a smirk across her face.

Violet passed her hand over the ID scanner on the desk. She was impressed by the woman in white's attire, by her status, and by her position in the Union, "Thank you! I'm... uh.... Estas honoro... ĉeesti... kun vi-"

The woman in white cut her off again, "Don't worry. You don't have to speak that anymore." She laughed at Violet.

She continued, "You've been selected for a very important task haven't you."

Violet replied, "Yes! And I can't wait! I've done everything I need to prepare -"

The woman in white's expression went blank, she looked over to her computer screen, "Yea, yea, I know, like I said. I've been watching you. Okay so you are... yep... apartment G732, district 30... from Naarm... height... age... yep... fully vaccinated... blood type-"

The woman in white then looked up at her, "That's the most important part huh?"

Violet smiled at her sheepishly. The woman in white then looked back at her screen, she continued, "Okay so… yep… anyway, how about we get you in there! All the attachments are ready! You're so special aren't you!" She laughed, side-eyeing her.

Violet was puzzled, *Why is she being so mean?*

"Yes sure, of course. Let's go!" Violet said excitedly.

The woman in white then pointed to the door without detaching her gaze. Violet headed over to it, which when entering, opened up into a long hallway, with a door at the far end too the right. This hallway, like that of the lobby, was sterile and painted an industrial white. Piping and cables lined it all the way down, complimented by unnatural light fixtures.

Not far in front of her she saw two men in full white attire. She began to make her way up to them. They signaled to an open door to left which led to a tiny concrete room. As she was approaching, she noticed that one of the pipes on the wall had slightly burst at one of the joins. Red hydraulic fluid was trickling slowly from underneath. She then approached the men.

"Hey, did you know you have a leak over there?"

One of them replied to her without changing their glance, "Yes we're aware."

They pointed to the small concrete room again. She looked up and noticed a plaque with some numbers on it; *19.9.13.21.18.7.8.* Violet then stepped inside only to be greeted by a small claustrophobic space. Mechanized tubes hanging from the ceiling. The hydraulic door behind her then slammed shut as she studied the contraptions. She could hear noises. Steam began filling the room. The mechanical tubing sprang to life and pulled her in close. Black grease began draping the walls. Startled, she calmed herself, "It's okay. It'll be fine... It'll be fine."

She tried to temper her breathing as two tendrils of the mechanized tubing arched up in front of her like snakes ready to strike. Looking at her like as if the machine was staring directly into her soul. They then pounced. She began to scream and flail about as they dug into her eyes. Mechanized electrical cables shot up from the ground and into her back and limbs, holding her in place. One mechanized wire, a syringe attachment on the end, then pierced through her forehead, before another identical wire pierced through her hand, snaking its way up the inside of her arm.

Outside, the two men began to walk off chuckling to each other. One of them looked down, "She was a different one wasn't she? not like the others..."

The other man in white responded jokingly as her screams echoed down the hallway, "Different alright, we didn't even have to do anything! I wish they were all like this..."

The two men continued to walk down towards the lobby, smiling to themselves as they passed by the red hydraulic leak, which was no longer a trickle, but instead, had now become a steady stream.

APORIC

# Aporic.

The elevator had almost come to a stop. Its exquisitely designed interior, matching the perfection of the lights. The luxurious aesthetic, complimenting the digitalized keypad on the wall. 223 looked down at his white attire, at the documents and tools in the many white pockets of his jacket. The scissors, the knives, the scalpels. The digital attachments, used to operate mechanical arms and various types of robotic tools. Everything he needed for work in the factories of the Megalith below. His heart rate started to rise. *I have to tell her what I really think. I'm not putting up with these working conditions. Those Biomechanoids are a stretch too far.*

The elevator came to a halt. The digital pad showing a flashing symbol of a golden triangle. He adjusted his white coat, making sure the folds were even, the buttons done up correctly. *They're just so dangerous. The robots aren't that good. But these things are too much. And if she doesn't agree? Then maybe that's the final straw, maybe I'll leave the Megalith. Escape this place… Get to the Catacombs… I don't know if I could though.*

The doors to the elevator began to open as he reached the top of Viscerum's Megalith. On the other side of the elevator doors, a wide-open concrete expanse. Perfectly sterile. The odd large wiring and metal piping sets could be seen in organised yet irregular patterns, snaking their way around the brutalist formations beyond. The area itself, immense. Stretching what seemed to be a mile above. At that height, it seemed to have its own cloud formations, very thin ones, made out of what looked to be faint dust. Almost perfectly still.

To his sides, odd brutalistic shapes and corners. Concrete formations of unnatural and strange shapes. Rooms that were rooms yet not rooms. That seemed to have a purpose, yet the purpose wasn't clear. Like a giant unfinished maze. The different open concrete levels possibly numbering beyond thousands.

A giant cathedral of barrenness. Of darkness. With the occasional ray of sunlight trying to get in from odd angles. The large wall to his left sloped slightly in towards him. Its height gargantuan, large irregular windows made from a crystal-clear glass let in the sunlight from the pure blue sky.

In a small outcropping of the wall beyond was a set of tubing and wires within a niche, facing a small window. He started walking over to it. Fixated on the figure within the wires. The sound of his boots gently echoed throughout the barren cathedral. Its empty concrete soaking up any other noise. He passed through a brief ray of sunlight, noticing the sparkle throughout the air, the sparkle of faint dust particles.

He reached the figure in the wires, calling out to it, "Chair Simurgh... I'm sorry to disturb you, but I need to bring something to your attention."

The eyes of the figure immediately opened. Its head and body attached to many wires and tubing. Some of the mechanical tubing began to detach and snake away from it. The figure's head began to move, focusing in on 223. A robotic yet humanoid woman. Her red lipstick and grey hair apparent. Her elderly yet youthful appearance, slightly obscured under a veil of shade. She began to speak, "What? What is it?"

"Mam, I... I just want to bring something to your attention... a problem..."

She began to separate from the wall in the outcropping, steam flailing about as wires detached and fell down. Her limbs becoming mobile. She stood up out of the wall, a frown crossing her face, staring him down, "What problem, what are you talking about."

223 stood up straight, he cleared his throat, "Well, It's the Biomechanoids. They just aren't-"

Simurgh cut him off, "The Biomechanoids? What's the problem? You can't accept change? Do you know what civilisation is based on?"

"Yes mam, I realize that, but-"

Simurgh looked out the window of the outcropping and into the bright blue sky. The endless expanse. A sea of clouds beneath them as far as the eye could see. She walked over to the glass, "But nothing. You'll adapt to the Biomechanoids. That's what the Union wants. So I'll make sure that's what they get."

"Yes mam, sorry, it's just that the rest of us in our section of the factory, and many other parts, have had trouble adapting our work processes to them. The robots have always been a problem, we all know that. And I realize they are outdated, but we know how to use them. They help us to hold onto the subjects, to hold our equipment, they can use some of the larger circular saws better than us… But the uh… The Biomechanoids… You can't tell them to do anything. They have a mind of their own."

"Why do you care? Just let them do what they want and you just fill in the rest. This should make life easier for you. They're doing most of the heavy lifting for you."

84

"Yes, but they also make decisions for themselves. For instance, one of them, and this is a report from the factory over, one of them actually grabbed one of our workers and placed him on the conveyor belt instead of the subject. It then started to form and shape him... The flaying and vivisecting done to the actual worker... Not the subject."

Simurgh looked at him, a look of derision, "Maybe that worker should have done his job properly then and it wouldn't have happened? The Biomechanoids are automatons. They're not digital. But they are perfectly made. If you can't farm those subjects effectively, then what is the point of you? The Biomechanoids act instinctively, maybe that worker should have done his job correctly. Why do you think they're being introduced in the first place?"

He was puzzled at her detachment, her lack of compassion, "Mam... The workers... the Union always prioritizes the needs of the worker over the task at hand. These working conditions are simply-"

Simurgh cut him off, "What? Simply what?"

He didn't reply, his eyes widened, his heart sank. *She couldn't care less about us.* His emotions started to build, but he tried to remain professional. Then, something caught his eye from outside the window. A bird. Some kind of raven, entirely black. It was flying up from out of the clouds. Its perfect jet-black feathering, reflecting a strange golden hue.

Simurgh watched the bird. She began to quietly mumble to herself, as if in a trance, "The cloud seeders, the Icarites. They need repairs. I know you love them. I know, darling."

Lightning periodically lit up the sea of clouds below. Simurgh continued to stare out the glass window, watching the small silhouette of an Icarite in the storm, "The crop has already been fumigated, repairs will have to wait, we need those resources elsewhere."

She focused back in on 223, her tone now serious, like one of authority, "We gave you a task. You didn't ask questions. Now all of a sudden you're curious. Don't you know what curiosity does to a man?"

"Yes mam, it ruins them."

"It perverts their character. It makes them something they're not. Is this world divided? On the surface it is. You know that. But up here? It's all in unison. Unity.

The Union. Order out of chaos. Did you see some chaos?"

*How does she know I know what the surface is like?* He thought to himself. *How does she know I was questioning the Union?*

"Mam... I'm not questioning the Union..."

"You think we don't track everything you do? Everything that everyone does? We have eyes everywhere. You know about the world below."

He didn't respond for a moment, his heart began to race, "...Yes. I know about what it's like down there."

"You were born here, 223, You've lived your whole life in the Megalith. You've never actually travelled anywhere. That was just injections and VR. I know everything there is to know about you."

223 began to open up with her, knowing what might be about to happen to him, his palms began to sweat, his voice shaky, "Then why is it like this... Why... Why are they being-"

"Why now does it matter? Compared to everything else you've done. You were happy to climb the ladder before, but once you get to the top suddenly you want a change in direction? What do you think the purpose of this world is?"

"To ensure equity and fairness for all."

"Yes I know, but what is the real purpose?"

"Peace, Safety, Progress, Sustainability. "

"Try again."

"Too improve, too adapt, too-"

"Too evolve. That is the purpose. To become something better. Something greater. To reach for the stars. To reach the clouds. To go above the clouds. Everything has a purpose. The Megaliths look chaotic, the world city looks chaotic, but overall it works perfectly. Zooming in on an anthill you might see an ant being dismantled by the other ants around it. Seems chaotic. But when you zoom out, you see that the anthill is thriving. That they're expanding. That they're improving. That's exactly what you've seen. Civilisation being perfected. Evolution."

He looked down. His hands shaking. The air was gentle, the perfect temperature. The sun was warm against his skin. The dust in the rays, like the echoes of angels. The clouds below, calming.

He spoke calmly, a hint of defeat, "…I just don't understand. I'm sorry… But I don't get why it needs to be achieved in this way. Those Biomechanoids… And not even them, why did that worker have to die? Why?... Why do they all have to die? Even the subjects?"

Simurgh continued to look out into the distance, listening to him, he continued, "The turbines mam… The turbines… I see them in my sleep. I'm so used to them, yet I'm not. The people… Just dropped into them from above… The screams in the distance as they fall. How their screams suddenly end. The sound of the wind being dragged down into the tube… It's not the flaying or the deforming that gets me. It's not the prolonging of their pain, or the fear in their faces… it's the turbines. The futility of it all. How insignificant each person becomes. How their screams suddenly end."

Simurgh responded, a calm tone, listening to him intently, "Subjects. They're called subjects."

Simurgh continued to stare out the window towards the vast expanse of clouds beneath them. Her focus resolute. Her gaze determined. She spoke calmly, "Before the skies were covered in missiles, people used to have to make decisions for themselves... After the missiles?... They began to have faith in the Union... Sometimes a few bombs need to be dropped before great things can happen. Do you understand?"

He continued to look down, his body trembling. Simurgh continued, "You're thinking too much... and not looking around you. What is there to want or care for? We have turned the world into heaven. Perfectly organized. Perfection. A world city. A Panopticonia... do you know what that means?"

"...No? what?"

"It's our world, Earth, our perfectly organized system. From here the World Union can see everything. All the World City. We can shut any door we wish, and open any door we choose. Move the Icarites, reroute the pipes. We can shut down entire districts at a time, or increase power in others. To give people a life of bliss, or nudge them closer in line with Union standards. Maybe a few limbs are lost every now and then, but the system as a whole remains the same. Working in organized perfection. As per our design."

"I… I think I understand now… I'm… I'm sorry Mam…"

He reached his arm out again and ran his hands slowly through the glistening particles, focusing in on the beauty. On the sparkle. The way the particles danced gently around him.

Simurgh then slapped his arm with force, throwing him off balance. Shocked, he reeled back, Simurgh screamed at him, "Stop fucking touching that!"

"Ow! Why?! What's wrong?! What did I do?!"

"Don't touch it! Just don't look at it!"

"Why?!"

"Just stop fucking touching it!"

Simurgh returned to her original pose. Panting with rage. Staring out the window. 223's heart rate climbed. *What was that about? Why can't I touch the dust?*

"I'm sorry I just was looking at the dust, it just looks so- "

She lashed out at him, shoving him, "I know what it looks like! Stop touching it! I'm well aware!"

Even though he was larger than her, he recoiled in fear, covering his arms across his body, "I'm sorry! What... What's wrong with the dust?"

She started slapping him and shoving him, her eyes wide with pure rage, "It's not dust! It's sand!"

A drip. And then another drip. Simurgh's expression quickly turned from anger to fear, she slowly looked up at the ceiling whilst 223 looked down to the ground just behind her. Red droplets on the abrasive concrete floor. Simurgh quickly spun around to view it.

"Look at what you've done!"

She then pulled out a part of herself, A small mechanical part, that began to extend, it fashioned itself into a thin cleaning device.

223 stared at the red liquid dropping from the ceiling onto the floor, "What is that? Is that blood?"

Simurgh continued trying to sweep up the blood, "You keep asking questions. You keep trying to change things that don't need to be changed. Obviously they don't like that."

Simurgh continued, mumbling too herself, "It's okay, It's okay."

He looked up to the dripping as something was coming out of the ceiling, "What is that!?"

Above him, in between the brutalist formations, was a singular red appendage, like a tentacle, trying to reach its way down towards them.

Simurgh whispered to herself as she continued to mop up the droplets, "You need to have faith in the Union... Violet."

223 stepped back slowly. *What is she talking about? What is that thing coming out of the roof?* Another droplet, off to his side. *What is going on here?* Then another some ten metres away from him. Then another red tentacle like appendage slowly began sliding out of an irregular formation at the top of an internal wall. Simurgh started following each droplet, trying to clean them up.

Bewildered, he watched as she kept muttering to herself, "Violet, darling. It's okay. Just look away."

223 spoke up, "Right. You're going to have to explain this to me. What are those things?"

She yelled back, frantically mopping up the blood droppings, darting about the place, "Did I not already explain to you! Civilisation works like an ant colony!"

"Yes I get that. So what is that?"

"What the workers work for!"

More drips were seen all about. Coming down from every corner, up in ceiling formations, out of irregularities in the concrete. He looked over to one of the tentacles as it recoiled. Bending back in a way which made it look familiar. Like as if it had bones inside it. Like as if it had an elbow joint. It was stirring up the air surrounding it.

He followed Simurgh as she ran from puddle to puddle, "What is it doing?"

"Don't worry about it. You should have just done your job. Now you've gone and stirred them up. I'm still cleaning this place, it's not ready yet."

223 focused in on the recoiling tentacles as it pulled back into the crevasse which it came out of, leaving a course trail of blood. Like a red sludge with the texture of sandpaper. A bird cawed off in the distance, the sound echoing throughout the cavernous interior. Simurgh threw her cleaning device down at the ground in a fit of rage, before immediately attempting to calm herself, "Violet! I told you not to look darling! Go somewhere else!"

223 was shocked by what he was watching, he thought about the strangeness of it all. How her mood changed.

Then he remembered what she said before. *It's not dust. It's sand.*

He turned to Simurgh and asked her directly, "What's wrong with the sand?"

She stopped what she was doing, slowly turning around to face him, as if on an axis. The cold stare of the emotionless robotic yet humanoid eyes, unnerving. The shadows cast down upon her face, hostile. Her bright red lipstick, like blood. Her grey hair, one with the surrounds, "I've had teams work on it. It's just an anomaly. That's all. Don't worry about it."

"No, there's something wrong with the dust... the sand... something's not right."

She tilted her head up in derision, looking down her nose at him, placing her hands on her hips, "I think it's time you fuck off. How about that. You're clearly not suited to be here. You can join the rest of them in the Panopticon. You don't realize how good you had it up here. There is a reason why we don't ask questions."

She pointed up at the tentacle in the ceiling, not breaking her gaze from him, "They know what's best for us.

Enjoy living with the shadow figures or whatever. Hope you know Esperanto."

*I'm so dead. There's no way she'll actually let me leave. Something is so off.* He thought to himself before replying, "Okay then. I'll go. I'm sorry if I offended you... And I'm sorry if I offended the Union... I guess not everyone is cut out for every task. I'll support the Union in my own way down there... I... I hope you will forgive me."

She scoffed at him before turning around, going back to sweeping and mopping the blood off the ground. With each stroke, smearing it further into the concrete. Staining it. Mixing it with the sandy surface.

He then looked up one last time at the slowly moving tentacles of gore and bone, before he turned around. Heading towards the elevator. *I'm not going to survive this. They won't let me out. I won't get to the bottom of the Megalith. The drones will be here soon. I know it.*

The closer he got to the elevator, the faster his heart beat. Behind him he heard the grinding of concrete, like as if a slab was opening. His mind imagined the sound of drones flying towards him.

He was then stricken with fear as he uncontrollably dashed for the elevator, not knowing what might be sent after him. Feeling as if he wanted to scream but having no time to do so. He could feel himself becoming hysterical as his dash turned into a sprint. He wanted to cry but he couldn't. It felt as though he was living in a nightmare. The sprint, taking an eternity. As though he would never reach the elevator. Like as if he was stuck in one place. Yet all of a sudden he reached the elevator doors, racing inside, before typing on the digital pad, as the doors shut. He collapsed to the floor and began to cry as his emotions finally destroyed him. He had no idea what he was doing or why. He was failing to fully grasp what just happened, yet felt as though he did. *Did I do the right thing? I just ruined my whole life. I just needed to bring that issue to her attention. I've gone and ruined everything. What have I done? I should have just done my job.*

He wished it would all be over. *Is it really just a case of looking at the bigger picture?... Or have we just become animals?* He screamed and yelled as loud as he could, hoping it would make the pain go away. He punched the elevator wall. Once, twice, three times. All before bounding himself up tight in the fetal position. Feeling like a terrified child.

The trip down should have felt like an eternity, yet only felt like a few minutes, as he finally reached the ground floor. The doors opened. Dark, pure black, except for the sparking of broken white lights. Office desks and rubbish thrown about the place. He shook in terror, listening out for the drones. All he could hear was the flickering of broken lights. He had to take this opportunity to escape. He jumped up and sprinted out the doors and through a dark and decrepit lobby. Pipes hanging everywhere, tattered chairs and lounges about the place. Thick black grease and oil dripped from the ceiling. Broken, sparking wires, dangled above. Pot plants with no plants. Reception desks damaged and worn. As he sprinted through the large lobby he tripped and fell over a broken chair and crashed down onto the ground. As he pulled himself up, battered and bruised, he briefly looked around his surroundings. No technology besides infrastructure. More old lighting that barely worked. Old appliances smashed. Nothing digital. But also... No people. ...*What happened down here?*

He continued sprinting through the lobby towards the outside world, as he did so, ramming into the glass doors in front of him, which didn't open automatically, and so he accidentally smashed straight through the glass. Again pulling himself up, even more battered, he continued on but noticed the extent of the destruction outside.

The lower portions of the skyscrapers around him were all run down. The lights were barely working. The Esperanto text on the neon signage were all missing letters. Neon building lights barely functioning. Clothes dangling from broken glass windows. He slowed down his movements as he observed the true destruction in front of him, a world he never knew of. Not from in the megaliths, not from above the clouds, not from anything he ever saw in VR. A shock to his system, a shock to his understanding of the surface.

There were no people at first, but he did notice some shadowy figures slowly appearing from dark places and from around corners. All wearing dark black attire. Hoods over their heads, their faces where covered in shadows. 223, knowing how out of place he must look with his now tattered white attire, blood and bruises all over him, began sprinting again. Jumping over puddles of black liquid and over tubing and wires of all sorts. He ran down a road that was completely full of more haphazard pipework and wires, that looked like it opened onto a clearing through the maze of skyscrapers.

There he then jumped onto a large black pipe, the width of two men. He began running down it, an utter emotional wreck. He kept running. The extent of this logistical network becoming clear, like a highway of giant pipes. The entire ground cleared out. An immense field of pipes all darting off in different directions. He noticed he was still incredibly high off the ground. *Is this even the surface? Where is the surface?*

He continued running, he looked back and noticed the ground floor was not the ground floor at all. All the skyscrapers continued to descend all around him. The area before him, merely a platform of dirt and rocks infused with manmade constructions and the foundations of buildings. He had no idea where he was. He couldn't even see the ground. Below the giant pipe he was running on, the ground opened up to reveal a mass ravine of dirt and rock, littered with large openings where the old underground subway systems used to operate.

He just kept running. His fears less about the drones, the Union, or the Shadow figures, and now more so on the height he was at, and the round surface of the pipe he was running on. Looking up, he saw more and more of these large pipes, all heading back towards Viscerum's Megalith. All the pipes as large or larger than the one he was running on. He began to slow down as his heart sank to the lowest it ever had. He paused and stared at a join in one of the pipes in the distance. It was leaking a red liquid. As two shadowy figures stood there, the taller one with a bowl of some kind, holding it up to collect the red liquid. *All these pipes… It's all… The whole world is… The rest of the Megaliths… They're all the same...*

He slowly looked around him at the rest of the hundreds of pipes, they were all in just as much disrepair, and they all leaked red. His vision started to blur again, and he felt his knees getting heavy as he noticed a few more dark shadowy figures on another distant pipe, staring at him, another bowl in one of their hands. He began to faint, collapsing to his knees, before noticing one of the shadow figures crawling up on all fours from around that same distant pipe from before. The taller shadow figure then leant down, placing the bowl on the ground. The shadowy figure on all fours began to lap up the red liquid before noticing 223 and turning to view him. Its lips retracted, revealed an abnormally large array of sharp teeth. Its mouth half the size of its disfigured face.

NON-EUCLIDEA

# Non - Euclidea.

"And then he woke up!" He heard Violet declare as she started laughing. Rostam began to open his eyes. "Wake up silly, it was all just a dream!" She began to laugh more as she leant over him whilst pulling funny faces. "Wakey wakey!"

He opened his eyes, the glare from the bright sun painfully obvious. "It was not a dream. Shut up. I told you I'm done."

She replied whilst pulling a fake sad face, "Yea, okay, It's not a dream. But I want to make you feel better somehow!" She then began to smile again.

Rostam slowly pulled himself up and noticed he had fallen asleep on a sun lounger. All around him a large pool area, filled to the brim with happy families and laughing children. Blue and white loungers everywhere, beach towels strung about. In front of him, a large glistening pool, incredibly inviting, the cold of the water being felt like an aura radiating from it, in pleasant contrast to the mild heat of the Mediterranean sun.

"I just want out. I don't want to hear his story again. I hate his story the most. It scares me to the core. You scare me to the core. I don't want to hear my story again either. But his is horrible. I told you I'm done. I told you I'm sick of this. Yet you keep bringing me back here to this miserable place. I want out." He grabbed his thick brown jacket from off the lounger and sat up.

She bounced up straight, placing her hands on her hips and pulled another fake face. Her pink top glistening slightly in the sun, her skirt moving slightly in the breeze.

He continued, "Your friend Simurgh. In all the times we've played over that recording, you've never said a word about her telling you not to look."

She laughed, "What? Are we supposed to be analysing our own history? You know that's not a part of our job description."

He looked at her with derision, "Do you ever think outside the box? Or are you just a slave to the system? The elite are entirely corrupted. How much longer until there's nothing left down there? Then what? The World Union has destroyed everything it's touched."

Violet replied, exasperated, looking off into the distance, "C'mon Rostam, don't exaggerate…"

"You know full well I'm not exaggerating. They're not human."

"You don't mean that. They are human. They're just more evolved than us, more advanced. Don't over analyse things too much. You and me, together, they chose us for this, that's what matters, and you know it. So… lighten up!"

His eyes still adjusting to the sun, "Yea, they chose us for this, but I never chose this. You're brainwashed."

He placed his feet on the warm open aggregate concrete. The pebbles shining a wide variety of beautiful earthy colours. He then grabbed his socks and brown boots and began to put them on. As he did so, noticing that his feet were perfectly clean. *A large pool area, outdoors, hot, yet not a speck of sand. Why am I not surprised.*

"How about we go for a walk." Violet said, trying to comfort him.

"Yep. Sure."

They began to walk out of the pool area, happy families passing by. He noticed a group of people were crowding around the entrance, flashing lights lit up the already bright area. Violet paced over to them, waving and blowing kisses at them. Striking poses and spinning around. The crowd desperately called out to her, craving her attention, "Violet! Violet! Over here! Violet!... Violet how do you do it?"

Violet responded to one of the paparazzi, "Look, you just don't understand what it's like to be me..."

The man was astonished, "Wow! That's one of the most profound things I've ever heard!"

"Violet! Violet! Over here, Violet!... Those things you said about the shadow figures, are they true?"

Violet flicked her hair, before striking another pose, "Yes they're true, and I'm proud of it, and if that administration bitch has anything to say about it, then you know from my research, that's publicly available by the way, that she is a fucking whore. Thank you for your attention to this matter."

"Astonishing! Write that down! Write that down!"

Rostam muttered to her as he began to barge through the crowd, "Get over yourself Violet, you live in a fantasy world."

A frown crossed her face, before she then proceeded to follow him out of the pool area and towards an open walkway. People were walking all along the clean and well maintained path, laughing and smiling. Families handing each other fairy floss and sodas. Telling each other jokes as they go about their business. Laughing amongst themselves. Some more dedicated tourists were holding cameras and taking pictures of the sights they saw. The paparazzi following them, kept their distance, respecting their privacy. Trees and shrubs sparsely lined the area. With small paths leading off to rides and attractions. All of the surrounds, an exciting yet relaxing amusement park.

As they began walking along the path, Rostam looked up at the roller coasters in the distance. Radiating a peaceful ambience of noise and laughter.

Violet looked at him after thinking for a moment, "Hey look, I know you don't like what you've seen. I know that... But where we are now is what truly matters. It's what we make of it, this world. I wish you'd understand why I do what I do."

Rostam scoffed at her, "Whatever. You might know what you do, but I have no consciousness of what I do. I have no idea which door I open, which drone I fly, which turbine I spin."

Violet, distracting him, grabbed him by the arm and pulled him towards a ride to the left, "Why don't we go on this ride! Come on!"

Dragging him over, he looked at the entrance. Vibrant coloured lights lit up the open entranceway. The red ribbons that straddled the archway danced in the breeze. Laughter is heard from the area beyond. Heading through the entrance, children of all the same height and dressed in white outfits, hop in an orderly line as they passed underneath the red ribbon archway.

Rostam yanked his arm out from under her grip, "No! leave me alone! Don't touch me!"

He then turned to the right instead, towards a coffee shop with an open bar under a large undercover area filled with chairs and people relaxing and eating food. On one side, a small open area where families were dancing and laughing as they listen to a live musician. At the bar, a brown-haired woman in typical barista attire, darting back and forth preparing orders. He approached the barista, planting his hands firmly onto the bar. Visibly stressed.

"You look like you could use a coffee." The barista said as she was pouring a drink. Smirking at him.

"Yes, I definitely could." He said, "Two shots, two sugars."

"Okay, no problem."

Something then caught Rostam's eye, he looked up to the wall, a calendar with dates crossed off, a picture of a cat playing with red yarn, he observed the year, *2733*. Anger started to build. He rubbed his eyes in shock. *She has kept me watching that recording for over a hundred years... I can't... I can't believe this is happening... I need to get out of here...*

Violet, now standing next to him, awkwardly smiled at both of them, "Okay, well I'm gonna go dance for a bit, come get me when you're ready." She then cheerfully headed off to where some of the people were dancing. *Everything she does is so forced, so fake. Is she even human anymore?... Am I even human?... I have to be. I feel like I am. But I don't think she is. She must just be a program. Singularity in her time must have removed the human aspect. It's like talking to a wall.*

He observed the counter, perfectly clean. The lighting fixtures above, perfectly aligned. The barista turned to him as she was preparing his coffee, "You know, I don't know how you too are even together."

He locked eyes with her, "You're not real."

The barista laughed, "Uh huh."

He continued, "… And we're not together."

The barista smirked, "So what, she's just dragging you around for no reason? C'mon..."

She then handed him his coffee. He looked down at the cup, puzzled, "I'm sorry, I think you gave me the wrong one."

"No that's yours, see, it says Violet."

"What? You know that's not my name."

The barista looked at him with a stern expression, "Yes. It is."

Rostam didn't know what to say. *How can she get that wrong?* He thought. The barista wasn't moving. Completely lifeless. Frozen in place.

He waved his hand in front of her, "Hey, that's not my coffee."

She responded, "Oh! Yes! Sorry, my bad!"

She then turned around to face Violet who was still dancing with the others. Her hair playfully thrashing about, complimenting the frills of her skirt. Rostam, confused, watched.

"Violet!" The barista called out. "Your coffee's ready sweety!"

Violet stopped dancing and yelled back, "Okay! I'm coming!"

Rostam's expression grew cold. *She didn't notice?* His blood began to boil. Anger started to build. *She wasn't supposed to do that. Something is off. Something is broken.*

He looked back over to Violet as she jovially skipped towards them, smiling at the people she was passing.

Rostam casually turned and exited the area, disappearing through a crowd, heading left and down the path. Passing as close to the shrubs and the edges of the buildings as he could. He kept his head down and puffed his collar up against his neck.

As he was about to turn a corner, he heard Violet yell out from behind, "Hey! Where are you going!"

He darted around the corner, turning right to start walking down another large path with more dense shrubs. In-between some he noticed a tourist sitting on a bench with a blue jacket, smiling up at the sky as he watched some birds fly above. Rostam quickly approached him and grabbed him by the neck. The

114

tourist visibly in terror, wide eyed. Rostam yanked at his jacket, pulling it off him before quickly taking his off.

"Put this on."

He placed his brown jacket over the tourist's shoulders. Seamlessly putting on the tourists' blue jacket as he continued power walking, passing another corner, and weaving through a thick crowd of laughing families. Paparazzi raced towards the direction he came from.

Rostam then saw a small back-door on a building between an alley. Inconspicuously placed. A broom and a bucket laying next to it. Rostam headed directly for it. He lifted up the bucket and picked up a small rusted key from underneath. He finally got the door open and entered an access hall for the workers of the amusement park. He locked the door behind him.

Inside, silence, every move he made echoed very slightly. He took the blue jacket off and placed it on a coat rack. Walking down the slightly dirty access hall. To his left he saw his destination. A white run-down door leading to a small janitors closet. A small dusty plaque was above the door with some numbers on it. He entered the room, closing the door behind him. In front of him, a small desk with empty noodle cups and soda bottles lying about an old computer. The monitor was large, it's screen bulbous. It's off-white colour, indicating its age. Around the desk, mops, tools and a large assortment of random items needed for cleaning and maintenance. Above it, a large painting of a picturesque scene, a grassy green park with an empty bench in the middle, surrounded by black birds eating seeds. But then he heard a noise from beside him where a curtain was. A curtain that was covering a solid wall.

It rustled as the shape of a person began to push through it. A woman appeared from out of the curtain. Rostam froze in place, ready to sprint back out the door. The woman had dark brown hair and barista attire. She was covered in dust, as if she had been between the curtain and the solid wall for quite some time. She had porcelain skin, looking as though she had died a long time ago. She stood still and stared into his eyes. He noticed her eyes were not normal, but instead, were black with lines of code in them.

"You're the barista."

She replied in a digitalized tone, "Yes."

He didn't speak for a moment. Contemplating the woman, her lifeless eyes, her unmoving body. He looked over at the computer, it was also covered in the same dust that she was, and to the same extent. *She's some sort of avatar.*

He looked back into her lifeless eyes. *Okay so something's wrong. I knew it was inevitable. Just a matter of time... Now... How do I get out of here... The factory I came from probably doesn't exist anymore.*

He spoke to her, "Where is the microchip factory that I was created in?"

She replied, her eyes flashing, her tone robotic, digitally fazing in and out, "That factory no longer exists"

"What is there now?"

"The area in that district is occupied by three residential skyscrapers."

"Where is the nearest singularity point?"

"Your location does not exist."

*Yea... I suppose it doesn't...* He walked over to the computer and sat down in the dusty chair, it creaked as he did so. He sat back. Tapping the armrest with his fingers. The hum of the computer in his ears. *I gotta figure this out...*

The barista moved over next to him, walking in an abnormal way. It faced the wall, before turning it's body and head around to stare at him again, leaning in towards him like a mannequin, a ventriloquist doll. He could see the code in it's eyes, each line, contrasting with the porcelain skin and the dust still falling off it.

He continued with his queries whilst looking directly forwards, avoiding eye contact with it, it's uncanniness disturbing, "Where is the nearest singularity point to Viscerum?"

"The Singularity Initiative is no longer operational. If you like, I can explain more about the Human Ascendance Initiative?"

*No that's useless, that's to do with the farms... I just need to find a body... Wait... Actually, that could work..,*

"What is the status of the Megalith at Viscerum? It's operations."

*"The Megalith at Viscerum is currently operating normally."*

*Strange...* He lent back in the chair. *Unless that glitch was just random? Civilisation has to be collapsing by now? It just doesn't make sense...* The barista was still staring at him, leaning in towards him, motionless, lifeless. He observed the painting of the park bench, the trees, the peaceful green park, this time, completely lacking of birds. He sat back upright. *That painting... It wasn't random.*

"The Human Ascendance Initiative, is there anyone hooked up to it in Viscerum currently?"

Her robotic tone cut in and out, *"There are currently 11,632,326 subjects attached to the HAI system in the Megalith at Viscerum."*

"How many are not being processed?"

*"0."*

"How many workers have access to the HAI system?"

119

"There are currently no World Union workers in Viscerum."

*Then how is it operational? No government workers? This doesn't make sense... wait...*

"What about the other Megaliths? How many are operational?"

"24% of the total number of Megaliths are operational worldwide."

"What happened to the nonfunctional ones? Why aren't they operational?"

The barista didn't reply. Still leaning in towards him like a statue. Her eyes then flashed briefly. She tilted her head.

"General wear and tear."

"What about the subjects? Where are the subjects in the disrepaired Megaliths?"

"Some of the subjects have been relocated to Megaliths closer to Viscerum."

"Some? Some are still there?"

"No."

"Where are they?"

*"*Many subjects are now residing in the abandoned subway tunnels.*"*

*There must still be rebels in the catacombs... Probably useless to me. Wait... Biomechanoids... That's right, the replacements...*

"How many Biomechanoids are currently under construction in Viscerum?"

"There are currently 668,490 Biomechanoids under construction in Viscerum."

"Are they connected to the HAI?"

"Biomechanoids are autonomous units which exclusively operate both mechanically and biologically. They have no access to the HAI."

Rostam let out a loud groan before slamming his hands down on the desk. *I have no idea how to get out of here... This is bullshit...* He then placed his head into his hands, resting his eyes. *I just wanna get out...*

He looked over at a book laying down on the desk, covered in dust and buried underneath a coffee cup and some old papers. He pulled it closer to him, brushing away the dust from the title; "*On SiO2 and it's consequences.*" His eyes lit up. He immediately sat up straight. *The Red Wire! I'm sure that's still operational... It's some sort of VR pleasure lounge or something now... There must be a body there... Wait... Where's Simurgh?*

"What is the location of Simurgh?"

The barista replied, "The location of Simurgh is currently unknown."

"What was her last known location?"

"Why are you snooping?"

Rostam's heart skipped a beat. He sat back in his chair, pushing himself away from the barista, staring at it's black eyes. A hum growing louder, ringing through his ears. Scanlines in the barista's eyes began to flicker. He looked over to the door and listened. Total silence. He looked back at the painting of the sandcastle on the beach. He slowly got up out of his chair, the head of the barista tracked his every movement.

He continued, cautiously, "I said… What is the location of Simurgh?"

The barista smirked at him, "Maybe she's enjoying that nice cup of coffee you left with me?"

Rostam then dashed away from her, smashing into a cabinet, rushing for the door. He struggled to open it, its rickety construction leaving it partially jammed. He shook it as hard as he could, vibrating the interior, and knocking the painting of the sandcastle with cascading waves closing in on it to the ground. The barista was now standing directly beside him, smiling at him, a deathly smile, as she reached out to grab him.

The door opened. In a rush he quickly went to grab his coat, tearing a part of his shirt off that the barista had gripped. As he looked at the coat, he noticed it was now brown again. And not only that, the entrance to the access hall that he first came through was no longer a door, but was now another solid wall with a curtain covering it. He put on his coat anyway before running down to the end of the hallway, which had an old door to the right. As he grabbed the handle he heard her footsteps powering towards him from down the hallway, coming from the computer room.

"Where are you going?" Violet yelled out, wearing her fancy black attire that was allocated to her back in Naarm, yet entirely covered in dust like the barista was. He briefly looked back as he was sprinting, Violet was trailing after him, he fell into a mad panic.

Violet called out again as she pursued, "There's too many of them, Rostam."

He turned back again briefly, yelling to her, confused, "What?"

"They are the problem."

"Who?"

"There's too many of them. Shadow figures. They damage the environment."

Rostam screamed back at her, panting, "Fuck off! Your masters do!"

She screamed back, now sprinting like him, "They're your masters too!"

He reached the door. *I don't know how to get out of here.* He thought to himself. He opened the old door and entered the room. Another hallway appeared, half the size of the previous, almost identical to the one before it, painted white with only a small identical old door at the end to the right again. He raced over to it and opened it. As he entered this next hallway, he noticed it looked the same again. And here there was another old door to the right. *I've never seen this place before.* He then sprinted to that door as well and entered it. Another room, an identical hallway, with, again, a door to the right. He paused for a moment. All he could hear was the flickering of the old ceiling lights. *…Something's very broken.*

He started walking slowly towards the door after closing the one behind him. But then he stopped for a moment and thought about his surroundings. There was total silence besides a faint electrical humming, and the slight flickering of ceiling lights. He turned to look at the door he just came from. Now contemplating where he's been, instead of where he's going. He then walked towards the next door. Slowly opening it. On the other side, another identical hallway. At the end of the hallway, a woman, dressed in black, hair covering her face. Her hair began to part as she lifted her head up.

"You're supposed to just do your job." Her voice cut through him like a knife.

"You went too far this time." She declared.

Rostam stared back at her. Not knowing what to do. Thinking of any possible escape.

He called out to her, "What are you gonna do? Kill me? You wouldn't go against the Union."

Violet snapped back, "Are you sure about that?"

Rostam began to shake. His palms covered in sweat. *Why would she say that? Has something really changed?* She wasn't moving. Her gaze like that of a lioness. Then

126

something caught his eye. He looked to the wall next to her. Particles in the air, like dust, began slowly spinning in a small vortex, localising towards her watch.

"Violet, look at your watch."

"No. You should've just done your job, I'm done dealing with you."

A distant pipe burst, spewing oil all over the corridor.

She continued, "Why do I need you if all you do is go against the Union's orders? I'll just do the logistics myself."

He replied, "Well obviously you can't though. Why would I be here if the government didn't want me to be here? Wouldn't they have already arrested me? Switched me off?"

"Life would be easier without you."

"You can't harm me, and you know it. You're not good enough to do anything yourself. You're vain. A puppet of the Union."

The hall began to shake, dust was turned up in the air, small lights in the ceiling began to shatter. Another pipe burst, spewing out water.

Rostam continued, "You know you're not allowed to do anything. You would never dare turn on your master. You've become just like her."

Her size began to enlarge, her hair standing on end, lengthening, moving in individualised clusters like snakes. An unnatural presence, clouding in from around her. Rostam looked back at her watch again, as its hands, spinning like that of a turbine, began deforming the world around it.

He continued, "You're just like that materialist bitch Simurgh, who sold her soul for a few bucks."

Violet let out a tremendous scream, shock waves shook every particle in the area, fazing in and out parts of their surrounds from existence. Flames began radiating from her sides, like that of fiery wings. The void closing in, like hands coming out of Hades. He tried to run but the ground cracked beneath his feet. He fell slightly and tried to regain his balance. He looked back at Violet, standing there, staring at him, dematerialising her surrounds, forming into a ball of light in the darkness, an entity of pure rage. Then the ground broke even more, and he fell through, grasping at the broken concrete and rebar of the floor as he fell. He couldn't grip anything. He was in free fall. The wind in his ears the only thing he could hear. He could see the structure above fading off into the distance, and noticed that it was just the hallway. Outside of that, an endless, bright blue sky with bright white wisps of gentle clouds. Very quickly, the room began to fall out of sight as he kept falling through the endless blue. He turned to face the ground as he fell, seeing a green field below quickly approaching. He shut his eyes and crashed into the grass.

When he opened his eyes, he noticed he was fine. The grass was soft. He looked around him, he was on a grassy hill that led up to a beautifully painted, small, white, simply styled house, common of many centuries ago. Around that, nothing but blue sky and white clouds. No roads, no trees, nothing. Just the grassy hill, the small white house, and the sky. The hill was tall yet sloped gently. The grass perfect and vibrant. The horizon was met at the pinnacle of the hill, where the house was. About 100 metres in front of him, Creating a stark contrast between the perfectly green grass and the perfectly blue sky.

He stood up and patted himself off, noticing that he was okay. He then paused for a moment. Thinking. Before slowly walking up the gentle sloping gradient.

An immensely loud voice bellowed out from behind the hill, "Man, oh man, oh man..."

He then froze in place, trying to figure out what it was. Then, a giant woman started to lift her head up from behind the hill where the house was. Violet. Straight and well-maintained brown hair, and a pink top, looking exactly the same as when he first woke up, except scaled up many times in size. She smiled as she slowly raised herself up from behind the hill. Only the top half of her visible, the rest obscured by the horizon of the hill. Rostam was stricken with fear as he noticed she was about twenty times larger than the house, making the house look like that of a dollhouse.

She slowly paused before smiling at him, her enormity reducing her speed. Her voice bellowed out again as she calmly addressed Rostam, "You keep trying, and you keep failing... I don't know how many times we have to go through this..."

Rostam then looked down at the grass. Terrified. Exhausted. Defeated. Broken. She continued, "All we need to do is be the custodians of knowledge... And to govern and control this world for the World Union... This is such an important task... It's not given to those who can't do it... they've given us one of the best jobs in the world. We can't die, we don't need anything, we just work and then we do what we want... We can't say the same for those down there... Do you really want to be one of them?"

Violet then slowly changed her expression to a smirk, looking down her nose at him, before she leant in over the house, "Look, how about this... we continue where we left off, but afterwards, we spend more time here then we usually do, okay?"

She looked down towards the house and opened the door gently with the tips of two of her fingers, her hand much larger than the door. Inside, Rostam, in his thick brown winter clothing. His boots off. Laying back in a recliner, with attachments protruding from his arms, and a VR headset over his face. Violet, in her normal size, is seen inside in her full black fancy attire, slightly dancing around and smiling to herself. Her paintings, filled with scenes of Naarm and various Icarites, lined the walls of the living room. She then waltzed up to him and held out a bowl of red liquid. He then took his headset off and smiled at her, before drinking from the bowl whilst she held it.

Violet then lifted her enormous hand away from the house and slowly looked back at Rostam, another smirk building up on her face. Rostam looked away from the house and what he saw inside to gaze down at his brown boots. They were covered in concrete dust and slightly torn. The grass around his boots gently rustling in the breeze.

*She still doesn't know who I am. She just goes off what she's told… Completely brainwashed… Delusional… She can't be a real person…*

In a monotone voice, Rostam responded, "I just want it to stop."

He paused for a moment, observing the grass swaying gently in the breeze, before continuing, "And I want it to stop for them too. How many more of them are gonna die? Eventually you won't be able to coax them onto the Icarites anymore."

"Yes we will. We'll just tell them they're going to space or something. Their VR and injections will make them think they're flying to another planet."

"Yea. Until they're placed on the conveyor belts... I just want it all to end. I just want to leave."

Violet looked concerned, she leant in closer towards him, "It's… It's what the Union wants. They know what's best... Look, the world is like an ant colony, from up close you may see one ant being torn apart-"

He cut her off, "Yes... Violet... I know..."

He noticed his hand had small grazes on it, the small amount of blood in the cuts contrasting to the white concrete dust covering his skin.

He continued, "Okay... Then show me the latest... Not a recording of hundreds of years ago... I want to see what's actually happening down there right now."

Violet began to smile and slowly leant back up straight. The sound of her clothes rustling in the breeze much louder than the surrounding environment.

He reiterated, "But I don't think this is gonna last... Violet... One way or another, our servers will stop operating. Civilisation will collapse. We'll have to escape somehow... The elite just can't sustain this..."

"What? That's impossible silly! Sustainability is one of our core principles!"

Rostam continued, "And the thing about the bee's or whatever, yea I agree, the world is like a beehive, but even if it seems to work from the outside, there could still be an unseen problem lurking within."

Violet looked confused, "What? Beehive? Ant colony I said. If you look at an ant colony. There are no bees anymore. They don't like the chemclouds. Do you ever actually listen?"

COLLAPSE

# Collapse.

A dripping was heard in the darkness. It's faint echo, giving a vague idea of where it was coming from. The air was thick and damp. Every once in a while, skittering and chittering was heard from beyond. Reverberating off of unseen walls and pipework. In the pitch black, a creature on all fours, was slowly making its way towards the sound of the dripping liquid. Unable to see, it carefully avoided rubble, rocks, wires and shards of metal with its sense of smell and hearing, using these in unison as a form of echolocation. The dripping was getting louder as it got closer. It paused for a moment and sniffed around in the air, making sure the coast was clear, before continuing on through the pitch black. Its hands and feet, both with long sharp claws, acted like paws, as it trotted its way through the darkness.

It noticed that it had now come across some sort of train line, considering the feeling of the terrain under its feet. It then trotted along the sleepers at an even pace before transferring onto the rail. Pacing along it, one paw after the other, with feline precision. Ahead, the source of the dripping was close. And a faint light was peering out from a place well up above, revealing ever so slightly, the dilapidated subway tunnel that the creature was in. It finally reached the place where the drips were pooling. A small puddle, it only held a few mouthfuls of liquid. Taking the opportunity, it quickly lapped up the puddle, ingesting along with it all the mud and oil that was mixed in. It tasted like a mix of water, biomass, and petroleum. It had a distinctive chemical burn after-taste, mixed with a hint of rust. But this was nowhere near enough to quench its thirst, or its hunger.

Then it pricked its head up as it heard the sound of something falling in the far distance. Its echoes revealing its general direction. The creature looked into the pitch black for a moment, not seeing or hearing anything else. It then let out one loud bark. It echoed throughout the darkness. It waited for a moment before hearing what it had feared the most... A loud, shrill, monstrous scream from the darkness beyond. Followed by the ever-increasing sound of fast paced pitter pattering of pawlike hands and feet galloping towards it. The creature began hissing and arched its back out of pure terror before dashing for the wall next to it. Using its claws, it clung onto any crack or crevice it possibly could as it scaled up it, heading towards a small crack in the concrete above where the light source was coming from. When it reached it, it slid itself through the tiny opening like a snake and climbed out the other side.

Reaching the bottom of this new area, it noticed that this place was incredibly large. Larger than it had ever seen before. The creature tilted its head in curiosity from side to side as it observed the room. An enormous cylindrical area, going up farther than the eye could see. The dark orange glow of the sun lit up the area above sparsely, piercing through damaged openings in the giant concrete tube, where dust clouds gathered. The only thing breaking its vision of the unending construction above, an immensely large turbine with blades bigger than anything it could have ever imagined. All dilapidated, all in disrepair. Covered in rust and sand. It wasn't moving, but it was creaking slightly. The low sounds of the cast iron creaks, echoed throughout this giant cylindrical interior, filling the ambience. As it looked around, it noticed wildly differing creatures hanging from the blades above. All mummified. All still. Stuck in their final resting places. Hanging from the blades like dark red ribbons. A crow pecked at one of the dangling remains hanging from the giant turbine.

The creature then looked down to the large open floor around it. Bits of rubble, sporadic piles of sand and dust, and the mummified remains of more humanoid-like creatures, all of varying shapes and sizes. It began to wag its tail and dashed over to one of them, munching down on it with excitement. Tearing and thrashing. Struggling to chew its jerky like meat. Crunching down on its brittle bones. But eventually, it had its fill. And began to lay down in the dust. Panting heavily with fulfilment. As it was looking around, it became curious about the light source above. The sunlight coming out of the large area. A single pipe scaling up from the ground and passing through this gap in the gargantuan concrete tube. Gusts of wind, gently blowing in more of the sand from above. The creature's curiosity got the better of it. It got up and started climbing the rusty cast iron pipe.

Once it entered the area above, it tilted its head in curious awe. This was something it had never seen before. Its eyes barely adjusting to the sun. Its mind running rampant with questions. A massive cityscape, giant skyscrapers everywhere, but all in disarray. Sand lined the streets. Most of the skyscrapers were half destroyed. One in the distance had collapsed completely over the street, taking down a part of another skyscraper across from it. The metal skeleton of a destroyed Icarite was protruding out of one of the ruined skyscrapers, having crashed there long ago. No artificial lights, no electricity, no sounds, besides the sandy wind wisping throughout the ruined cityscape. A rusted out Icarite was slowly drifting through the sky above in the far-off distance, parts of it damaged. It's cloud ports, sputtering and struggling. As its eyes adjusted, it noticed that the sunlight was partially blocked out by the sand in the air above. But it was still reasonably bright. The world around it, off tones of orange and red from the sand and the sun, imprinting itself on the grey concrete and rebar rubble surrounds.

The creature, excited by the prospect of exploring this new environment, set off down the sand covered street, only stopping to sniff the air and any object worth investigating. To its side, the opening to what used to be some sort of large shopping area. The creature went in through the doorway where double doors used to be. The area was largely open and covered in sand, mostly destroyed. In the middle, a ruined escalator going up to the next level, but the next level was completely open, most of the floor and outer wall had collapsed, letting in more sunlight and sand. But off in a corner behind the escalator, another small puddle. The creature dashed over to the puddle in a mad gallop. Wiggling its body from side to side as it couldn't contain its excitement. It lapped up the puddle, about two times larger than the last. This time, it was mostly water mixed with a smaller amount of oil. The taste refreshing and soothing. But this wasn't to last.

Another noise in the distance startled the creature. It was the sound of glass being crushed under the weight of something. The creature immediately spun around to look at the entrance it came through and started growling. There, in the entrance, a shadowy figure. A man in full black attire, with a black hood over his face. His face draped in shadows. He stood there and stared at the creature. His hood, hiding his intentions.

The creature began to slowly back up into the corner and continued to growl. The shadow figure then started to slowly walk towards it, crunching glass and sand with every footstep. The creature started barking, and began to tremble. The shadow figure, slowly getting closer, had reached behind his back, carefully pulling out what looked like a large, dark-coloured firearm. The creature then began to bark in a more high-pitched tone and scrambled against the floor, pressing itself further into the corner, knowing it couldn't climb away, as the ceiling above didn't have an avenue for escape, the way to the broken section obscured. The shadowy figure was now closing in on the creature. Holding his arms out slightly, with his gun in one hand. The creature then began yelping and screaming out in pure terror as the shadowy figure called out to it.

"Tio estas bona knabo, vi estas sekura...."

The creature, now screaming, formed tears around its eyes.

The shadow figure called out to it again, this time in a more soothing tone, "Tio estas bona knabo, vi estas sekura..."

The creature stopped screaming and froze for a moment as it stared at the shadow figure. It's heart racing. It listened in again, but this time, trying its best to understand him.

"That's a good boy... You're okay...", The person repeated again, this time, even more calmly, as he stretched his arms out towards it.

Understanding what he was saying, the creature then stopped pressing itself into the corner and patiently observed him, deciphering his intentions.

The person, now directly in front of the creature, tried to comfort it, "Hey... hey boy... it's okay... don't worry, I have something for you."

The person reached down into his pocket with his free hand and pulled out a piece of food. A sort of jerky, but the smell was not like anything it had ever smelt before. Curious, the creature slowly approached the person before gently eating the food out of his hand. It was delicious. The creature started to become happy as he pulled out another piece for it. The creature then began to wag its tail and lick at the person's black sand and dust covered cloak.

"That's a good boy, come on, we have a lot of ground to cover. You're gonna be a big help to me. I'm a hunter, but I'm not hunting you. I'm hunting something else. Don't worry boy." The Hunter patted its head.

He then turned around and proceeded to leave the area and head back out onto the street, constantly looking behind him to make sure the creature was still following. The creature couldn't believe its luck, its eyes fixated on the Hunter, mesmerized by him. Out on the street they maneuvered over sections of rubble and climbed up small sand mounds. Up ahead, they turned the corner and began heading down another destroyed street. This one, very long and much wider, possibly once being a main road through the city. It led off far into the distance. All around it, partially collapsed skyscrapers.

The Hunter then began to talk to the creature as they continued to walk down the sandy street, "Here, I'll show you something."

He then put his gun away and stopped walking. Fumbling around in his black coat, he pulled out two polaroid pictures. They were faded, but mostly visible.

"So..." He knelt down, leaning in towards the creature.

"So this is what I'm hunting. These two. You see these two people here?" The creature tilted its head in curiosity as it carefully analyzed the images.

"These two have caused me a lot of distress. You don't need to know the details... and I suppose maybe you wouldn't understand... but these two... I need to take them out."

The creature looked up at The Hunter before looking back down at the images again. The first polaroid image showed two shadowy figures, both men in dark attire, black hoods over their heads, but in this image, their faces were visible. In the other image. What looked like one of the same shadowy figures holding onto a chain attached to the neck of a crying child, dressed in black tattered rags, as he reached out towards something out of frame. The Hunter then reached into his pocket again. Pulling out a black tattered rag.

"Here, see what you can pick up from this."

He held the rag in front of the creature's nose, it began to sniff it. Pulling the rag away slightly, the creature darted his gaze to lock eyes with the hunter before then staring directly in front of him. It then sniffed the air for a moment and started trotting off in front.

The Hunter sighed with relief, "Well okay... alright... better than I expected..."

The Hunter then stood up. He followed the creature as it led in a haphazard manner over rubble and sand piles, sniffing various objects and areas. It then paused for a moment and looked into an abandoned lobby. The broken sign above it barely reading the words: *la Ruĝa Drato*

Inside was dark. A reception desk to the left, covered in dust and sand, and stripped bare. To the right and in front, a silent area filled with old loungers, all in disrepair and covered in dust. Above each lounger was many tubes and wires, hanging eerily still, stuck in time. Still attached to some were needles in their respective brackets. some broken, with more needles and attachments missing from their sockets. The broken remains of VR headsets littering the ground, partially buried. They navigated their way through the quiet and dark area. With the creature leading the way through the maze of contraptions. Eventually they reached a small backroom, the door was laying on the floor, partially buried. Going into this room, there was a small section of collapsed wall, where a window once was, with sunshine shining through, highlighting the stillness of the dust particles floating through the air. Outside, a large open area where most of the skyscrapers had collapsed entirely, surrounding a gargantuan crater in the ground where a skyscraper had completely given way, exposing the many hundreds of subway tunnels and access lines crisscrossing the underground world. Rebar sticking up from piles of rubble, with a crow perched atop one. Then a cracking sound was heard. The Hunter screamed out in pain. The creature quickly turned around to see what was wrong.

"... It's alright boy... just..."

The Hunter huddled into a dark corner of the room as the sun began to set, "This happens all the time... don't worry."

He knelt down slowly, before laying back against the wall. The creature, curious, walked up to him and began sniffing and licking his face and body.

"Get back. Lay down."

Exasperated, he tried to get himself in a comfortable position and gazed off through the broken window to watch the night set in as the creature curled up next to him.

"You know... I never expected you to take to me so quickly... the catacombs must have been rough on you huh?..."

The creature, still curled up next to him, lifted its head and laid it on the hunters lap, gazing into his eyes.

He continued, "At least you've never had to deal with a Biomechanoid. They usually don't go down there. Once they set eyes on someone it's basically all over... Even though they don't have any that is..."

The Hunter smiled, yet the smile didn't reach his eyes. The creature tilted its head in curiosity once again, listening in to the Hunter, trusting every word he said, memorizing his voice, his facial tics, his mannerisms.

"Just, if you do see one… just run, I will too. We probably won't though. They usually stay in the Megaliths. They're red, like bare flesh, no skin… and they shake. The most dangerous things I've ever seen."

The hunter began to pat its head, "I'd hate to think what happens to them in the Megaliths. The people that is. What a world we live in, huh? One minute everything's great, all the biomass in the world, water that doesn't burn your throat… The next? …It's all taken from you… Captured by some selfish shadow figure, sold for allotments, handed over to the Biomechanoids..."

The creature continued to watch the hunter, his every eye movement fascinating. The Hunter continued, "It really doesn't have to be like this you know... it just doesn't. Everyone is so angry. Always. All the time. Everyone is more interested in a quick fix instead of a long-term solution… At least I actually tried. Nobody seems to care though..."

The hunter looked down for a moment before reaching into his pocket and pulling out a tiny pouch, "This here is what people don't understand. We used to have thousands of these. I spent a lot of time trying to find them. You can talk to some people, and they'll tell you tales about a time when the world was better."

He began to open the pouch, the creature watching his every move. Gently, with the tips of two of his fingers, he pulled out a minuscule dark brown object.

"This here… is a seed. They grow into food. They're plants. Clean, soft, and full of water. It doesn't look like it would, but it does, I've seen it."

The crow perched atop the rebar outside twitched, briefly catching the Hunters attention, its head gently drooping, looking as though it was about to fall asleep. He focused back in on the seed, "I suppose you wouldn't know, being from the Catacombs, but in the ancient days there were many of these, and all in groups. Forests, they called them. Which was like a city of plants… But then there was the time of chaos... They say each People's Republic was hit with over ten thousand missiles each. But luckily, just when it looked like the end, the World Union saved humanity with the help of the Phoenix, and started building the world city."

Exhaling, he spoke under his breathe, "And that's great... but now there's no forests left anymore... I just wish they saved some."

He began to roll the seed gently between his fingers as the weight of the world began to crush down on him, "I've only ever had two of these. They're nearly impossible to find. No one believes me when I tell them about what it does, but it's true. I got the other one to grow. I did everything right. I placed it in sand. I poured oil and water onto it every day. I drew all the right sigils around it, and in the right order. I blew concrete dust onto it every time a bird cawed. I even said all the right incantations. It did grow. It was bright green and the size of my hand. It was so soft and fragile."

He grasped the seed slightly tighter, "But then it died."

The creature watched him vehemently, every facial expression, every eye movement, every hand gesture. Then The Hunter gazed off through the window. The night just as silent as the day. The only noise, the wind wisping through the rubble and ruins outside.

"My leg is wrecked. I just want to do this one last job."

The hunter continued to gaze out before placing the seed back into its pouch and slowly shuffling down to lay flat on the sandy concrete floor with the creature then rearranging itself to curl up closer to him, as they both drifted off to sleep.

PERTURBATION

Alex James

# Perturbation.

Violet was watching the screen intently. The visage was shaky, the feed cutting in and out. She could see the creature underneath the broken turbine, chewing on the dried scraps of the creatures before it. On the screen next to it, very dark current footage, the visage seen from outside the broken window, the night making it hard to see, it showed the creature and the hunter fast asleep.

She turned around to view Rostam. Comatose and strapped to an inclined medical bed. Cords and wires all over him. He twitched every now and then. Many wires and tubes darted off in all directions. Each one connected to a screen or fixture of some kind.

*What am I gonna do with you.* She thought to herself. *I just wish you'd stop trying to rebel against us and just do your job. Maybe then we could improve you a bit. Maybe you'd be conscious of how you interact with the world then. You're old tech.*

She walked over close to the bed, leaning over him, she whispered to him, "Why..."

He lay there, unaware of her presence, silently watching the creature and the hunter as they slept. *Why are you like this*. She thought to herself. Her face half covered in shade, like a veil as the door slowly opened behind her. "... I'm not supposed to kill you... but sometimes you just-" She gathered herself, taming her frustration, and turned around to head outside.

Outside, a rickety metal railing, free from any rust marks. Beyond that, an enormous city. Skyscrapers all around, reaching up into the dark stormy clouds above. A light rain soothed the cityscape. The Icarites, all in perfect condition, free of shadow figures, glistened in the sky, slowly making their way towards their destinations. Clouds being formed around them as they drifted. A fresh metallic smell filled the air. Small drones carrying packages darted throughout the cityscape, a dull buzz emanating throughout the area. The lights from all the buildings around her, sparkling like stars. A distant billboard with bright neon lights flashed between three messages:

ELECTION DAY - TODAY!

VOTE 1# NAARM RED PARTY! "BECAUSE YOU DESERVE BETTER!"

VOTE 1# VICTORIAN BLUE PARTY! "BECAUSE YOU DESERVE MORE!"

She leant down on the railing, a smile across her face, the wind gently blowing through her hair. She began thinking to herself. *I love this place. The Icarites. The city. The choices. The lights. The colours. The rain. It's just so beautiful. I wouldn't want to be anywhere else.*

She watched as an Icarite gently drifted by her, reflecting the lights of her skyscraper on its giant hull.

*It's like a giant peaceful whale.* She felt calm, she slouched down further onto the railing. Enjoying the fresh oil and metal scented air. *Hey, remember when he once said that the World Union was actually in the business of causing chaos or division or something? Division I think it was.*

She replied to herself, "That's stupid. They're called the Union... As in unity..." She returned to her daydreaming. *Yea, Union, as in unity. How can they be causing division if they are literally named after unifying the world?*

"I know right... I know..."

Something then caught her eye. She looked over to the opposite railing. *Is that a person?* She focused in on it. A woman. A shadow figure. On one of the many hundreds of railings on the opposite skyscraper. She stood up straight, "Why is that here? I never allow shadow figures here?"

The shadow figure stared at her. It's tattered black attire rustling in the breeze. A chill went up Violet's spine. She watched as it began to move. It raised it's hand up slowly, holding a bowl. Its arm fully outstretched towards her. She snapped her fingers at it.

"Why won't it go away!" She yelled out in frustration.

She snapped her fingers at it again, "Go away!"

She looked down at her watch, the hands spinning rapidly.

"I said go away!" She continued snapping her fingers.

The shadow figure stood there. Staring at her. Arm outstretched with it's bowl. Before suddenly dematerializing.

*What is going on? Why did that happen?* She thought to herself. She looked at her watch, the hands now slowing down.

*Wait, didn't he say that the world was breaking or something?*

She scoffed, "I'm not entertaining that idea."

*Yea but it would make sense wouldn't it? Look at the world right now, it's pretty much in ruins. Only parts of the megaliths are still working. And it would explain the things like the barista and what I just saw, right?*

"It's not breaking. The Union would tell me if there was something wrong… and they haven't… so…"

*Yes but the world is in ruins, go into that room again and look at the screens if you don't believe me.*

Violet's frustration started to build, the veil of shade crossing her face again, "Stop. There's nothing wrong. Think about something else."

*Why do they eat their own people?*

"Shut up! There's nothing wrong!" Violet screamed out into the cityscape. The sound of glass shattering filled the surrounds. The airships all stopped in place.

*What does Viscerum look like right now?*

Violet grabbed her hair, scrunching her fingers together, digging them into her scalp. She let out a visceral groan.

"You wanna see? You really wanna see what it looks like? Okay I'll show you!"

She spun around and threw the door open, storming up to one of the screens as Rostam still lay comatose on the inclined bed. She grabbed a remote and pointed it at one of the screens, aggressively changing channels. Her hands shaking, her breathing rapid.

"See! Everything's fine! See!"

Screen after screen flashed by. One of a dark room with no one in it. One of a creature with odd appendages being sawn open by something out of frame. One of an interior with a collapsed concrete wall, rebar sticking out. One of the exterior, showing a massive blast crater stretching several levels. Another one of a dark room with no one in it. One of the city from a shattered ledge of the megalith, showing an endless sea of concrete and sand.

"It's fine! See! Like I said. Everything's fine!"

*It's not fine.*

"It's fine!"

*It's not fine.* She collapsed to the floor, planting her face into her palms, and began sobbing, "It's really not fine, is it?"

*No, not at all.*

"It really isn't..."

*So why is this happening? Maybe he's right about the Union, about the elite. If life is getting slowly worse over time, and yet they say that everything is working as planned, then maybe they're just lying?*

"That doesn't make any sense. Why would the government lie to me?"

*I don't know. Maybe because they have their own agenda. Maybe they're simply there to consume, regardless of what happens to others... even if that leads to the destruction of the world?*

"No... It just doesn't make any sense… Why would someone do that?"

*I don't know.* She slumped down further, the tears building up, her sobbing turned into crying, "Where's Simurgh?"

*It's not your fault.*

"Where is she?"

*I don't know. There's nothing you can do about that. I don't know where she is.*

"I just wish I could talk to her."

*I know.*

"I miss her..."

*I know darling.*

She looked down at her hands. The tears sparkling like diamonds, before evaporating in front of her. Another Icarite began passing by, a gentle gust of wind blowing into the room. She gathered herself and slowly stood up. Her head down, she walked back out to the balcony.

"They're no longer human... The elite... are they..."

*I don't think so. I don't know. They have their tentacles everywhere. It's been like this for centuries. They were human, a long time ago. I think technically they still are human. Like the creatures.*

"Evolved humans?"

*Maybe.*

She looked up at the cityscape, at the buildings, at the sights. She raised out her hand towards the clouds to her side. They began to part, revealing an enormous base of a megalith behind the skyscrapers, stretching up into the beyond, dwarfing the rest of the cityscape around her.

Out of the clouds appeared a giant version of herself, like that of a Titan, with a comforting smile, slowly making its way over to her. She smiled back at the Titan, and noticed the hands on her watch were ticking at a soothing pace.

"Look at that megalith though. It's unbelievable. How could anyone even make that? Who comes up with an idea like that? It blows my mind."

The Titan slowly turned to look at the megalith with a loving gaze, before beginning to caress it.

*It's truly amazing isn't it. The foundations are built in unison with it as it rises.*

"As above so below."

*Something like that. It's like the pinnacle of Panopticonia.*

"...It's beautiful …I can't imagine anything more amazing than this."

*You know... maybe it's not so bad? I mean, if they were able to come up with that, then they must be still worth fighting for? They perfected civilisation. Saved the world from destruction. I may not be able to understand them right now, but I have to trust them. I need to have faith in the Union.*

"I need to have faith in the Union."

*I need too. I really do. Look at this world. Maybe the real one is in bad shape right now, but if they could make the whole world as advanced and organised as this once before, then they must be able to do it again. It's just that their thought process is beyond me.*

"I need to have faith in the Union."

*I can't listen to him. He's trying to change me. They chose me for this. I should be more grateful. I hope they'll forgive me. I need to be more grateful for everything they've achieved, and for everything that surrounds me right now. They'll fix this. The ruins will be repaired. I know things will get better.*

"I need to have faith in the Union."

RUINS

# Ruins.

The distant sound of gunshots cracked sporadically amongst the ruins. Reverberating off of the rubble. The creature immediately jumped up and rushed over to the window to look out across the desolate cityscape. It began barking. Another distant shot cracked through the surrounds. The hunter jolted up and immediately grabbed a hold of his weapon, before rushing over to the window and carefully peering out.

"They're here."

He then backed away from the broken window, heading out towards the street. Walking over layers of sand in the long-deserted room, exiting through the main doorway. The door itself, having fallen apart long ago. He began making his way down the long sandy street. Rubble lined the way down. The street itself succumbing to desertification. The ruins of the concrete skyscrapers around him barely reflecting the orange glow of the endless sandstorm that had now set in above them. A never-ending landscape of concrete.

The hunter stopped and turned to the creature, "I can't hear them anymore boy. Where are they?"

He watched the creature with a stern yet determined expression as it sniffed around in the air. As it did so, he looked up into the sky and noticed the sandstorm above was picking up. A deceivingly distant roar being heard from the storm as it began to rip through the sandblasted and eroded pinnacles of the concrete skyscrapers. The area closest to the ground was like being in some sort of eye of the storm. A storm that could soon drift downwards towards them.

The creature then began to head down the street as the hunter followed behind it. It darted from pile to pile, under and over the broken concrete formations that cover the street. Making their way down, the creature suddenly stopped. The Hunter, almost out of breath, also stopped, starring at the creature. It turned around and looked at him before sitting down attentively.

"Okay. Good boy."

The Hunter noticed the large dune of sand on the street in front of him and headed towards it. The creature carefully following next to him. The Hunter then made himself prone, and crawled up to the top of the dune. Carefully peering over, he saw them...

Two shadowy figures, not far away, laughing to themselves and chatting. Beneath them, another person lies motionless on the ground. The breeze rustling their black and tattered attire ever so slightly as a black bird circles above. In the hand of one of the shadowy figures, a chain attached to a shackle around the neck of a small child. The child was looking down at the motionless body. The child's attire, more tattered and exposed than that of the two men.

The Hunter crawled back slightly and looked down at the sand. He whispered, talking to himself, "Okay... Okay I've gottem... What do I do now..."

The sandstorm well above them began to pick up. Seemingly getting lower. The hunter pulled his black robe further over his face, "I don't have much time... "

He looked around and continued thinking, as the creature copied his movements.

Watching the creature carefully, he signaled to it. The creature, watching him repeat the signal, then immediately turned around and darted off towards the ruins directly next to them. Sneaking its way up them like a snake, before disappearing through a small crack somewhere along a higher level.

The Hunter crawled up the mound once more and observed the men. Still in the same position, laughing and chatting amongst themselves. The child was still, like that of a statue, staring at the corpse on the ground. He then noticed a pile of rubble on the other side of the dune. He began to slowly get up, now crouching. Keeping his eyes fully locked onto his targets. He began to make his way over the mound and down to the rubble. Now at his new cover, he prepared to aim his weapon. He drew it up to his face and looked down its rusted sights as the figure holding the chain of the small child yanked it tighter. Pulling the child in next to him, and directly in front of the hunters sight. The Hunter could barely make out what the figure was saying, "Rekte Viscerum vi estas iranta!"

The shadowy figure then grabbed the child's hair and shook him about, before laughing and continuing to chat with the other man. The Hunter watched them like a hawk. Waiting for the right opportunity. The right moment. Finger on the trigger.

The shadow figure then pushed the child away again, making the child fumble before regaining balance. The chain now outstretched.

The street is then filled with deafening gunfire as the hunter unloads on the men. Startled, they instantly drop to the ground and cover their heads as the rubble and concrete around them is torn to shreds. Rocks and dust explode all over the area as they then jump up and run for cover in opposite directions.

"Damn!"

The Hunter quickly pulled back as return fire teared into his surroundings. Rocks ricocheted around him, his ears began to ring from the deafening gunfire. The firing now slowing down, he gathered himself, psyching himself up before sprinting out into the street, firing at both positions as he found new cover closer to them. The return fire tearing apart his new surroundings. Out of breath, he reloaded his weapon before peering out again and firing at the figure opposite to the one with the now crying child. the figure tried to fire back, peering slightly out around its cover. The Hunter fired, the figures head exploded into a mist of blood and bone. His lifeless body collapsing into the sand.

He aimed his weapon over at the last shadow figure but couldn't see him. Panting and shaking violently, the Hunter struggled to aim, waiting for the figure to peer out. For anything to happen.

The street fell silent. All he could hear was the sound of his panting, the sandstorm above, and the child crying in the broken doorway behind the rubble.

"C'mon... C'mon..."


The Hunter still shaking, quickly looked over to the cover where the now dead figure was, he whispered to himself, "Go... go..."


He then sprinted over to it. As he did so, gunfire tore into his surroundings, sand was thrown up and concrete ricocheted through the air. But when he reached his new cover he realized he made a mistake. The angle of it compared to the cover of the last remaining figure meant that he was exposed. Instantly, he knew he had to charge him or be shot. He immediately charged over towards the last shadow figure's position, firing frantically. The last shadow figure jumped up, startled, and raised his weapon to return fire.


The Hunter felt as though he had been hit with tremendous force. An immense ringing in his ears. He immediately fell to his knees. The shadow figure stared at him, still holding onto the chain of the child. The darkness cast over his face from its black, shadowy hood, began to envelope him, its sinister grin widened. The Hunter stared at him, his vision beginning to blur. The world seemingly coming to an end. Yet through the blur, he noticed movement on the concrete wall behind the figure. Another figure. Brownish in colour, yet almost camouflaged with its surrounds. Slowly snaking its way down until it was directly above the shadowy man. He watched the snake-like creature in his periphery, as it lurched up behind the figure, forming a terrifying face. A monstrous sight of teeth and bone. Its lips slowly revealing an uncanny array of incredibly sharp and elongated teeth. Its jaw, slowly becoming unhinged like a snake. The full size of its teeth and mouth, now dwarfing its skull in comparison.

It let out a horrifically shrill scream as it jettisoned itself from the wall and jumped onto the shadow figure, latching itself on to him with its claws and biting down on his skull. In one swift crunch, the entire top portion of the shadow figure's head was obliterated. It then began to psychotically rip into him. A flurry of movement, blood and bone being thrashed about the sand. In only a small amount of time, the shadowy figure was torn to shreds in a explosive mess.

The Hunter continued to watch as his vision began to worsen. He looked over at the child as it was staring off in the general direction of the carnage. No longer crying, but now silent and overwhelmed. The snake-like creature ended its attack and looked up at the Hunter. It regained its sanity and realised something was wrong. It slowly made its way over to The Hunter on all fours, worried about him, as blood dripped from its mouth.

The Hunter didn't break eye contact with the child. The creature began to sniff him as its teeth pulled back into its skull. The Hunter didn't say a word. Barely blinking. Only slightly breathing. The child then broke free from his trance, and finally noticed the Hunter. He stood up straight, and rushed over to him, the chain dragging behind as the boy began to cry. The Hunter struggled to stretch out his arm towards him, trying to comfort him. The creature looked over at the child as he approached, standing in front of The Hunter as his eyes began to close. The creature then sat down beside the little boy, as they both stared at the only person in the world who had ever cared about them.

NAARM

Alex James

# Naarm.

"That was a new one…"

Rostam was solemnly fixated on his glass. His eyes barely open, staring desolately into the reprieve of the sweet liquid. Enticing him to forget what he just saw. The sparkle of the glass like as if it were made out of diamonds. The perfectly sized cubes of ice dancing with the viscous dark orange liquid. A sweet smell gently wafting towards him. His jet black exquisitely crafted suit, the perfect comfort. But he wasn't focused on any of that. He was focused on the glass. On its unnatural perfection. On the world below. His voice was deep and slurred.

"I said, that was a new one."

Violet replied, "What was, hun?"

His eyes glanced over at her from under his heavy brow. His gaze like that of knives. She continued chopping for a moment, her sequin dress reflecting the many white lights of the black marble kitchen. Her hair waving and curling, as if supported by an unnatural presence.

She continued, "Oh that? Yea, it just happened. Sad really."

Her watch began to spin faster. He stared at her for a moment longer, slumping deeper into the soft black-leather couch.

"I didn't want to hear that one... Hun." He remarked sarcastically.

She didn't reply. He continued swishing the cubes around in his glass. The light periodically giving them a sandy appearance.

"I really didn't like that one very much..." He gripped the glass tighter.

She glanced over towards him and shrugged, timidly smiling, before quickly going back to what she was doing. The thuds of her knife on the board getting louder, the sparkling of the particles within the black marble counter becoming more pronounced.

He continued, "...I found out about the Second Great War, Violet... From before I was born..."

"Oh? And?"

Rostam's face scowled, "You know what happened."

Violet smiled at him, replying in a sweet and bubbly tone, "Only a little bit! It was a long time ago. Long before me too. And I don't think it was as bad as they say. No point dwelling on the past! You told me that!"

Rostam paused for a moment. Contemplating his surrounds. The glass in the living room. The knives on the counter. In the drawers. Hanging from hooks behind her. The thud of her knife into the chopping board. She kept cutting. Thud after thud into the impassable surface. He focused back in on her, clearing his throat, "The ground... it was covered in trenches. Every continent. Everywhere. The sun blacked out from the drone swarms. The only light, the flashes coming from the direct energy weapons, hitting the missiles."

"Wow... I love it when you bring up interesting historical factoids."

"Violet... Those trenches were manned by both men and women... and then pregnant women... and then eventually children. All conscripts. The lasers stopped the missiles. And the drone battles overhead ensured the stalemate. No one was supposed to win."

"Well, war can be like that, at least it ended before-"

Rostam cut her off, "You know exactly what ended that war. After all those years. After all those millions of deaths... The EMP strike."

"Lucky, so grateful for that."

"It disabled every direct energy weapon on Earth."

Violet had a slight shakiness to her voice, she started chopping at the board in front of her erratically, she began to stutter, "You see! people were trying to stop that horrible war! It was, like, the worst one in existence! You know? Imagine if all those lasers were pointed at the people instead! Wow, lucky."

Rostam, now sitting up straight, "After that, every single nation on Earth launched all of their missiles at the same time."

She began to yell as she pointed her knife at him,"No. No! That's just a revisionist historical, like, take, like, as in you're looking at the facts in the wrong way. It's malinformation- "

Rostam cut her off, "Violet. That EMP was developed by the World Institute for Unity."

"Yea! They saved humanity!"

"Violet..."

Violet immediately threw her knife into the sink next her, before haphazardly grabbing the board and everything on it and throwing it at a cabinet. Utensils went everywhere.

Violet, wide eyed, screamed at him, "What's your point! What do you want me to do about it!"

He declared, "I want you to give up this blind devotion you have to the Union! You know what happened after the missiles? The world powers just so happened to meet in a neutral place in the mountains... After that? The World Union suddenly appears and the World Institute for Unity-"

Violet cut him off, "So what? Who cares!"

Rostam continued, sighing, "- disappears... One World Union. One World Religion. One World Government. Everyone in the world just suddenly agreed on everything. Think about it."

"It literally doesn't matter! They saved humanity! They stopped the war! Don't you care about that? You only focus on the negative! They literally stopped the war!"

"They started the war, Violet! It was all planned. Even the name of the deity of the one world religion they made was called the Phoenix."

Violet began to calm herself, refusing eye contact for a moment, she started speaking softer, "So? It helped rebuild civilisation? You want to have a conversation about religion now too? Maybe she's real maybe she isn't. I don't know. Try prove it. Good luck."

"Violet, It was an orchestrated war. They killed off those who could resist their new system, or even question it. They prolonged the war. They then ended the war the way they planned too from the start. They got every single thing they wanted. If the people couldn't be kept in line with materialism after the fact, then they would be through their manufactured religion. And the deity of that religion is depicted as a woman holding a half crescent."

"So? What does that matter? The Phoenix brought them hope. The crescent symbolizes resilience and providence and stuff."

Rostam leant over closer towards her, speaking calmer, "Violet... It's literally just Simurgh holding a bowl of biomass. They tricked the world into worshiping their own AI."

Violet screamed back at him, "Stop hating on Simurgh! She's the nicest person I've ever met!"

"She's not real Violet. Even in your time she wasn't real. Maybe she was once. A long time ago, before the war. But she hasn't been real for many hundreds of years."

"Well if she's not real then you're not real either!"

"Correct. I'm not. And neither are you."

Violet reeled back, her face went blank, "Yes, I am."

"No. You're not."

Violet stared at him. Contemplating his directness. The words he was saying. Why he was saying them. She looked down at her hands, her sequin dress sparkling in the light, the hands on her watch spinning out of control.

She replied, a hint of sadness to her voice, "I am though... I am real."

Rostam sighed, leaning back against the couch, "No... Violet."

A tear began to form under her eye, "I am real. I'm me."

Rostam looked off at the city outside the glass wall window. The sparkling lights, the flashing propaganda billboards, the Icarites, "...I don't think so. I think we died a long time ago."

Violet tried to gather herself as one of the Icarites slowly drifted by. Clouds being peacefully formed from out of its hull like mist. The metallic smell filling the apartment. A strong sense of nostalgia washed over her. She remembered the city. What it felt like. The rattle of the exterior walkways. The sound of the cables above the elevators. The hum of the old orange lights. The crack of the lightning in the cityscape above. *I shouldn't listen to him. He's trying to change me.* She thought too herself. She then looked down her nose at him, derision in her voice, "No. I am real. Actually. And this place is real. Reality is what you make of it. If it was created, if you can comprehend it, then it's real."

"But it's not though. This isn't real."

"Define real then?"

He didn't say anything. With a smug grin, she continued, "Exactly. Your view of reality is problematic and outdated."

She took a sip of her wine, before he asked her a question, gazing out at the cityscape, "Fine. So where actually are we then?"

"Somewhere in the PRV."

He laughed, "The PRV huh. You mean the one that's now in ruins? The home of sustainability or something, right?"

She walked over towards the glass wall. Holding her head high, staring off towards a flashing propaganda billboard. Red neon lights reflecting off her face, she began to give a patriotic speech, "Yes. My home. Our home. The PRV. Naarm. Where everyone has an equal vote, and an equal stake. Where we remember the problems of our past in order to accurately address the present. Where the state provides us with access to all the information we need to make an informed decision about our future. A city of equal opportunity. Inclusively segregated. Where sustainability and untapped desires meet. Where all our medical needs are provided for free. Where even the clouds protect us from infectious diseases, blocking out the harmful rays of the sun. The freedom to go to your allocated profession with ease. A place of happiness. True happiness. There's nowhere quite like it. The greatest city in the World City. This is our future. This is our home. This is our Republic. The People's Republic of Victoria!"

She victoriously took another sip from her wine glass, proud of herself and her accomplishments, and proud of the city she grew up in. He then slowly stumbled up off the couch, making his way over to the large glass wall and positioning himself next to an old exquisitely designed chair. He looked out the window towards the sparkling abyss below. An abyss filled with both light and darkness, "The PRV. Awesome. Great."

He continued, his slurred tone now slightly louder, "A People's Republic! Ah yes, a Republic! Just like every other one! Freedom at last! PRV, PRA, PRNZ. Wow! There's so many unique places in the World Union! Yet they all look the same! The People's Republic of Victoria! Wow!"

She replied in a proud tone, "Yes. Naarm truly is magnificent."

He laughed, "You're beautiful, really stunning Violet, you're like the phoenix of the PRV! The pinnacle of Panopticonia! Wow! Come out and vote everyone! Come out and vote for your only fucking choice!" He threw his glass down at the ground, shattering it into thousands of diamonds, the liquid turning into sand.

He continued, "Where are we? Violet?"

She placed her hands on her hips and snapped back at him, "I already told you. The PRV. Naarm."

"No, what is this place."

"We're at home."

"Oh! Home!" He leant around to look over to the front door, "So uh… Where is the rust on the door handle?"

"That's enough."

"No rust particles on your fingers today? What about your mirror? Is there still a crack in it?"

"Oh for fuck's sake." She began to storm off.

"Where are you going Violet? I thought this was paradise? Isn't this fantasy worth it? This fantasy world? People are literally dying in front of our eyes. And we do nothing. But you have this fantasy world right? Your virtual reality isn't really reality is it?"

She snapped back, "We were tasked to do a job! To record! to interact! to-"

"To interact? When have we interacted? To open some doors? To re-route things? Some calculations? I don't understand? We calculate things? We're computers? We make Icarites move? I have no consciousness of this, you do. All I know is surveillance. Why aren't we interacting with the people down there who are being abused? Who are literally dying right in front of our eyes. But we just watch... That, what we just saw, was real Violet. That was fucking real. Interact? Why couldn't I interact with them? That little boy could've still had his father. That was the present. I could've spoken to them through a device or through the-"

"Because they don't want us to change the world! They want us to do our job! What do you want me to do? Go and save the shadow figures? Why? They won't even understand who we are? If we spoke to them they wouldn't even know what to do with the information we'd tell them! They'd probably think it was a god or demon or something!"

"So what about 223 then? We could have spoken to him back then? Oh but wait... That bitch was there wasn't she ... Wow Violet... Everything around us is a lie. Everything. We have no incentive to continue working for these abominations. They're not even human anymore."

"So? Neither are we, remember? And they're not abominations, they were elected! This is civilisation! It's not always nice, but it works-"

"What are you talking about? It doesn't work! Right now there is a little boy in chains walking around a fucking desert with a monster who has no idea how to fucking look after him and the boy is probably so traumatized-"

"Observe! That's it! And interact for the good of our civilisation when the Union wants it! We strive to serve the World Union, for all the People's Republics, for democracy!"

"Fucking hell girl, wake up! The fuck has democracy done for us? Wake up!" Rostam grabbed the exquisitely designed chair from beside him and began smashing it against the glass wall.

She crossed her arms, "Now what are you doing…"

He continued smashing it against the glass wall. Thud after thud, "I'm going to show you that time is running out."

She scoffed under her breath, "What? You're gonna jump? You can't break that, it's pretty strong."

The glass wall smashed, the shattering startled Violet. The wind immediately picked up and began to drown out any other noise from in the apartment. Violet started to move toward him, unnerved, "How did you... Why are you doing this! What do you think this is gonna change!"

He replied, "Everything!"

He then stood tall, facing her directly, and raised one arm out of the window as the strong loud winds blew his suit about. She focused on his movements, her heart rate increasing, her breathing becoming heavy.

"You're insane Violet! I don't know why! But I can prove it! I don't hate you! I just want you to wake up!"

She continued staring at him, trying to decipher him, trying to figure out how to control him, how to change him. In this moment he seemed to her, entirely uncaged. And a memory immediately filled her mind. She looked up at the old man sitting on his bench in the grassy green park, feeding the birds. One line reverberated with her as she cawed. *Birds born in cages think flying is unnatural.*

He opened his hand partially. Violet's watch was dangling from his fingers, she jolted toward him in a panic, her eyes wide with fear, "No! Stop! Don't do that! It'll be fine! Trust me!"

"It won't be fine! It's never been fine!" The winds began to pick up even more, seemingly trying to push Rostam back into the apartment, the sound almost becoming deafening, the watch in his hand still dangling.

"This is not reality! You need to break free from this system! Look around you! Our pleasures are fake! They mean nothing! The world is crumbling! It's a desert! Not this utopia you've made! You live in a fantasy world! You need to break free-"

She began to fall into hysterics, "Stop! Don't drop the watch!"

"It's not real! Stop me if it is! But you know you can't! There's two of us in this reality!"

She began to scream at him. Then a bright flash blinded him for a moment, he looked over at the dark city. One of the skyscrapers was hit with an explosion. Then another. The skyscrapers began slowly crumbling down. Screams echoing out from amongst the sound of the wind. The ground shaking.

"Those are rockets! …They're rockets aren't they! The Union isn't in control anymore Violet! You know this! Focus on what's real!"

An unnatural heat began to emanate from Violet, her screams becoming more ethereal, light began to build up behind her, he continued, "They're not in control anymore! It's just us! It's over! Civilisation has already collapsed! Viscerum has fallen! Wake up!"

He glanced at the watch, the hands had become a blur, spinning like the blades of a turbine, pulling in parts of the cityscape towards it, "It's time! Break free! Fuck the World Union!"

He then lurched back, firmly grasping the watch in his fist, before throwing it with all his might out towards the now chaotic and war-torn abyss of the cityscape. He looked over at Violet. Fear consumed him. The heat emanating from her was now unbearable, her size enlarged, Firey wings began forming from behind her, her body engulfed in flames, light shining through her eyes. Feathers of fire surrounding her beak. Her screams, like that of a thousand harpies. Then a burst of flame. Rostam crouched down and covered himself.

He tried to stand back up, but he noticed he couldn't. Suddenly, everything was black. He tried to move, but he felt that he was becoming stuck. The fire hadn't hurt him, yet his skin began to feel pain. At first a dull pain, but then, a sharp one. All over his body he felt tingling. He couldn't see anything. And now he couldn't move. He felt like a statue in the blackness. In the void. In the dark. He could hear a digital sound. But it would fade. Every now and then he thought he could see sparks, or maybe geometric shapes, but then it would return to black. He felt trapped. Yet he also felt... Real. Actually real. Something he hadn't felt since he was in the PRA. Since he was... alive...

# Human Farms.

Not a sound. No feeling. Just an empty void. Black nothingness. Was he dead? Was it over? The silence lingered. He began to wonder what had really happened. Every now and then his pulse would pick up, like as if fear was overcoming him. He could feel his blood move, yet he still couldn't see. As time passed, he wondered if he had made a mistake. If being in that apartment was actually where he belonged. *Am I dead?* This thought usually sent his body into a panic. But it would eventually pass.

Then something broke the silence. A noise coming from beside him in the distance. A buzzing. *What is that?* It was getting louder. Sporadic cracking sounds were heard as more and more industrial and unsettling noises filled the silence. The sounds of liquid splattering and distant cracking mixed with an industrial buzzing. Like some sort of circular saw. Then he realized something. His pulse began to pick up again. He felt he was slightly regaining control of his body. He moved one finger, it was painful. He could feel something sticking out of the side of his head. A tingling sensation. He then noticed the feeling of things sticking out of multiple parts of his body, pulsating, pushing and pulling at his insides. He felt even more trapped. He felt his eyelids twitch, but he didn't want to open his eyes. The tingling started to be equally met with pain as his heart rate started to increase even more. The beating was getting louder. *I need to open my eyes*, he thought to himself. And so... he did.

A dark, poorly lit wall was in front of him. Black pipework and random jolts of steam filled the area. Black grease draped the machinery, seemingly one with the opposing surfaces. The only other colour present, varying shades of red. He slowly tilted his head. Feeling as though it was stuck. He saw in front of him on the adjacent wall a badly mutilated humanoid, bare flesh, mostly skinless. It looked dead except for one eye which was slowly looking about the place in a trance. Most of its body covered in black tubes and wires, pulling and pushing at its internals.

The circular saw noise started again. He knew what it was cutting into. Screams then began echoing out around him. He wasn't far away from it. He tried to turn his head to see, but the more he tried, the more the apparatuses attached to him tugged and resisted. Eventually he observed it. A large partially robotic, partially humanoid creature was sawing at a farmed humanoid. Attached to its appendages, an array of saws and metal claws. Its face, a bare humanoid skull, its body awash in red gore. Vibrating like as if it was steam powered. Like as if it was a mix between a biological humanoid, and some sort of mechanical automaton. His heart rate was now at its max. He was breathing rapidly. Staring at the monstrous creature in fear.

Then Rostam let out an intense scream as all the pipes and wires attached to him began to detach and shoot off into the air, flailing about, spraying blood and dispersing steam everywhere. He tore out of the fleshy confines he was attached too and fell to the ground. The ground now covered in his own blood. Breathing heavily he looked at the floor for a moment before noticing the large biomechanical creature not too far beside him had stopped cutting. He stayed perfectly still. Only the sounds of the factory and the distant screams. He then turned his head again to look at it. And even though it had no eyes, he realised it was now staring directly at him.

He instantly jumped up and began sprinting away from it down the hall. He could hear the Biomechanoid pursuing him. The vibrating of its mechanical parts. The fleshy thuds of its heavy feet. In front of him, a decrepit railing, beyond that, what looked to be sunlight, yet his eyes were yet to adjust. But then, just before he reached the railing, he felt a sharp pain in his foot. He tripped over and quickly looked at it. However, he failed to find the damage that caused the pain, because his entire foot was covered in blood. It had no skin. He realised that the majority of his body had no skin. In a state of disarray he shunted himself back, trying to flee from a problem he couldn't possibly flee from. He slipped between the railing, and entered into a free fall, watching hopelessly as he fell down further and further, many floors below...

He opened his eyes and looked up above him. The world was still. It was quiet again. But he was breathing. He had fallen many stories. If it wasn't for the mess of pipes and ductwork strewn about the place, he would have surely died from the fall. They dangled gently above him, now damaged and torn, the dust stirred up, drifting in the breeze. He was now in a tremendous amount of pain. He continued to look up for sometime as he lay, watching the dust particles as they danced about the air gently.

But then he noticed something. There was an abnormal amount of sunlight in this area, everything was very well lit. This place was more grey then black, like as if the factory had been eroded back to its original concrete. But more strikingly, was how captivated by the sunlight he was in this eroded place. He looked around him and realised that from where he was, to about five stories above, was a massive hole in the megalith's exterior. Like as if it had been torn out. Blown to pieces a long time ago. Rebar and rubble strewn about the edges of it.

A large, motionless red tendril dangled outside from somewhere way above, the tip of it moving and curling ever so slightly. Like a giant tentacle. And then he noticed the light orange clouds beyond it. Intrigued, he slowly stood up in pain. And looked out at the world outside the Megalith. In total awe.

The sky was covered in what looked like a raging sandstorm. It expanded as far as the eye could see. Below it, an equally impressive sight. Thousands of kilometers of sand and grey coloured ruins. It stretched almost entirely to the horizon. Yet at the horizon the sight was slightly different... At that point it looked as though there were no ruins. Only a desert. Endless dunes. The distant wisps of sand, like waves, closing in on the remains of the city. Gazing back at the ruins of the skyscrapers below, he was especially mesmerized by their pinnacles. It seemed unnatural yet beautiful. Even though the sandstorm above was not reaching the ruins below, the tops of what was left of them looked as though they were being gently blown away. Like as if the ruins were as brittle as the sand itself. Yet as these structures were being gently and delicately blown away into the breeze, the particles that made up the dust seemed to shimmer and sparkle, refracting the light ever so slightly. It was both a beautiful and dreadful sight. A feeling he had never felt before.

Then something caught his attention in the corner of his eye, a small red tendril was curling up against the concrete ledge slightly. He turned to face it and observed that part of the wall, the ledge that separated the opening and the interior. Parts of the concrete were being blown away like dust, yet the breeze was calming. The tentacle moved slowly, trying to grip onto the remains of the exterior wall, yet the concrete slightly crumbled as it did so.

Curious, he walked over towards it. Trying to ignore the pain. Focused in on the one thing he had spent centuries trying to escape. The tendril barely moving. Trying to grip onto something solid, yet failing each time.

*You were never that strong, were you.* Rostam thought to himself.

The small tendril continued to desperately grip at the ruined concrete rubble. It's bare flesh being covered in dust. At times, it would flinch when accidentally touching a particle that was too gritty. It continued, timidly feeling around, like a small hand in the dark looking for a lightswitch. Rostam reached out and held the end of the soft tendril in his bare hand. It paused for a moment, seemingly shocked, before delicately moving about, confused as to what was holding onto it.

*You had your tentacles everywhere once. But no one realised just how soft those tentacles were. They thought you were formidable. Like a fortress. But you were always fragile. You're just a castle made of sand. The only thing that kept you in power was your facade. Even the smallest wave would have made you crumble... Why... Why didn't anyone stop you...*

He felt the tendril, how soft it was, how it flinched at every movement, how blind it was, how it struggled to understand what was going on around it. He then placed the tendril back down onto the rubble and looked at his hand. It had left concrete dust soaked into his flesh. Partially sparkling. Rubbing his fingers together, he could feel the grittiness. *Is it because of my exposed nerves that it feels so gritty? Or is this material actually soft?* This train of thought then made him notice the pain again. His whole body pulsating with an excruciating burning sensation.

He looked out once more as the sound of distant thunder distracted him. Peering out over the broken ledge, he saw a storm rolling in. The dark blue clouds being lit up from time to time by silent lighting strikes. Like as if the thunderstorm was about to compete with the space the sandstorm was occupying. Then, out of the clouds, he noticed a black dot flying towards him at record pace. It came closer and closer. Flapping it's wings. A bird. It dived in towards him at record speed. Now in full view, it let out a sharp caw as it stretched out its wings into a glide, the dust particles disturbed around its outstretched wings sparkled, briefly giving it a fiery appearance. It flew directly over his head and into the building. He ducked and spun around to watch where it was going. It flew straight through the area and down one of the dark, desolate hallways. He began looking around again at the vastness of this ruined space. *What had happened here?* He could hear creaks and groans, like as if the building itself was buckling under its own weight.

Another scream was heard. This time muffled and incredibly low in tone. It came from somewhere deep down in another corridor. Worried, the pain began to die down. He looked at his flayed hands and wondered how much longer he had left. He wondered if this was it. He wondered if he had made a mistake. If listening to Violet's story over and over again would have been a better fate than this. Then another noise was heard. Yet this one was different from anything else so far. A darker, lower, baritone roar. Seemingly a mix between a human scream and the bellow of a bull. Coming from somewhere deep down within the maze of the Megalith. He knew he had to move, and move now. Not knowing where to go, he started running toward the dark hallway that the bird flew into. Every step, painful, as his bare feet made contact with the grit of the concrete floor. He picked up the pace. The hallway he was now entering was barely lit. Some lights were present that helped him find the way. Periodically lighting up and shattering every time he entered a new area or turned a corner. The corridor was covered in thick black paint. Steam from small pumps lined the walls. Like as if the architecture had become organic. Like as if the megalith itself was part organic, part machine. The distinction between man, machine, and structure, blurred. He continued to traverse the buildings' black oily vein.

As he continued to make his way down he noticed a door to his left. This door was different. It looked like a shade of white. It was open slightly, and had a giant gouge in it and some scratches. Like as if a large circular saw had haphazardly cut into it. A black feather was stuck in one of the cracks on the side. The handle was smashed and laying in pieces on the sandy floor. He walked towards it, the door creaked as he pushed it open. Inside, a decrepit and dusty room. Some sort of old office. Modest in size. With lockers, desks, and a dusty computer. Stationary was laying about the place. Including some cups and a burnt-out painting. The entire room in shambles. He slowly walked around. He noticed a white lab coat on the ground. It was mostly torn, some of it seemingly shredded and spread about the place, with dark red blood stains. He walked over to the computer, curious whether it worked. He pressed the button to turn it on but no response. He tried again, but this time the button crumbled into sand. Curious, he wiped away the dust from the screen. It was incredibly thick. He paused for a moment and contemplated what to do.

He then walked around the room more and noticed a set of small concrete stairs leading downwards. He walked over to it and noticed it was well lit, and there was an ancient style telephone on the wall. It was colored a faded red, covered in dust, with a manual keypad and a phone that was attached to it with a red coiled wire. He walked down the stairs towards it. Watching the bare flesh of his legs ripple as he did so. The sound of his flesh, splattering on the concrete with every step. The clack of the bones in his feet, colliding with the concrete.

He then turned his head to see that the stairs continued down again off to his side. Only a small way before another door similar to the one he came through, this one also ajar and partially destroyed. He reached out and grabbed the phone. He pulled it to his ear. *A tone.* His head shot up. His heart began to pound again. He put the phone back then pulled it out again and listened. The tone again.

"Hello?" He called out in a panic.

"Hello? Can you hear me?" His breathing started to pick up.

"Hey, I was wrong! Violet? I want to come back now!" He was becoming panic stricken as he waited to hear something on the other side.

"Hello! Please! You can stop it now! I know this isn't real!" He listened for a moment before slamming the phone back in again and pulling it out.

"You can stop it now! I get it!" The dial tone rang through his ears.

He slammed it back in, but as he did so it started to ring, Startling him. The sound jarring and distorted. He picked it up again. This time, there was no dial tone... A static background noise.

"H-hello..." He said, then holding his breath, hoping for a response.

The digitalised voice of a girl replied, distorted and almost incomprehensible, "It's... real..."

"No, no, no... No it's not, please, I want to get out." Rostam started to pace back and forth, placing one hand on his head, like as if he was trying to grab onto hair that wasn't there.

The crackled and broken digitalised voice of the girl replied again, "You... Are... Out... It's... Real..."

He slammed his bare hand onto the wall, leaving a splattered red mark.

"This can't be, there must be a way out, tell me how to get out."

She replied "I'm... Sorry…"

"No! Get me out of the Megalith! Please! Violet! Just get me out!"

He stood still and listened. Pacing about. She took her time to reply.

"Down... The... Hall... Quick..."

He replied, "What am I looking for, where am I going?"

"Quick... Down... The... Hall... Quick..."

Then he heard a noise coming from the office room above. It was the sound of the door. Although he couldn't see it, he could hear the door creak slightly. His heart sank.

"Quick... Down… the… Hall…"

He brought the phone down from his ear as he looked up the small stairway. Trembling. His heart beating. He slowly put the phone back. Then he heard what he

thought was breathing. Slow, methodical, breathing.
Deep. Then footsteps, incredibly low thuds. His heart
now beating faster. Out of the darkness above, he saw
the dust on the ground kick up and drift down the stairs.
Then he saw something. A skull appeared slowly out of
the darkness. Vibrating. Covered in gore. It was staring
at him even though it had no eyes. The thuds continued
until it stood still at the top of the stairs. The heavy
breathing of a bull. A huge beast of blood and gore.
Shaking. Steam shooting off it sporadically. A grotesque
automaton of organics and metal.

Rostam instantly sprinted down the stairs beside him and
to the slightly ajar door. He slammed into it, breaking
through it, and ended up in another dark, black, hallway.
A corridor of metal, ribbed with pipes and contraptions.
To one side there was a T-junction. On the wall at the
junction, a bright red light shining onto the body of a
humanoid, splayed and vivisected, with a bird sitting on
what should be its shoulder, pecking into the humanoid's
eye socket. A metal tube was sticking out of its head,
Electrical sparks emanating.

Rostam bolted for the humanoid, eyeing the attachment
in its head. The Biomechanoid then careened down the
stairs and smashed into the black corridor, tearing off
pipelines and tangling them on one of its arms. Oil and
steam began spewing out, covering the corridor as the
beast corrected and charged at Rostam, tearing
everything off the walls as it did so. Rostam, now

reaching the humanoid, jumped up onto it and tore out the tube lodged in it's skull. Sending a spray of blood into the air. He then spun around and watched as the beast was almost at him. He felt around on his flayed head for the hole in which the tube could be attached, before finding it and plugging himself in.

# Desiccation.

He gasped for air, falling to the floor. The sand was coarse, the area dark. The sandy surrounds were littered in needles and wires. Contraptions of all kinds, dilapidated and in disrepair. He heard a thud into the ground beside him. Dust began to fill the small dilapidated concrete room.

The voice of a girl called out from beside him, "Ugh, are you serious… Yuck… There's sand in my mouth."

Rostam turned around to look at her, standing back up, his black tattered attire heavily draped around him. He watched as a dust covered woman also in tattered black attire began to rise out of the sand, dusting herself off. A frown across her face. He spoke to her, "Violet."

She turned to him, scowling, "Yes. Are you happy now?"

"Why are you here?"

"Oh, I don't know, maybe because you brought me here?"

"I didn't bring you here. You should have just let me go."

"Oh! Let you go! Do you know what I had to do to get you out of that Megalith? I'm gonna guess that the World Union is not too happy with me right now…"

"There is no World Union anymore. There's only the Biomechanoids in there."

"That's not what they told me."

Rostam sneered at her, "Uh huh." He then started to walk out of the ruined building.

He heard her griping to herself, still dusting herself off, "I'm a shadow figure now! Oh great! Thanks!"

Outside, the sandy city street continued all the way off into the distance. One way, the giant concrete Megalith, dust clouds drifting off from parts of its ruined exterior. The other way, more ruins as far as the eye could see, eventually leading into an expanse of sand dunes. The narrow street completely quiet besides the wisps of the sandy wind through the ruins of the once tall skyscrapers around them, now concrete and rebar husks. Rostam observed the sight of the Megalith, the gargantuan holes in it's exterior.

"What happened to it?"

Violet stumbled over towards him, frustrated by all the dust on her black tattered attire, "What? What is it?"

"The Megalith. Look at it."

She looked, shielding her face from a gust of sand, "Yea…"

Then she looked around, before continuing, "So uh… Where's all the people?"

He turned to her, "What people."

"The people, the stupid shadow figures, we gotta go find someone I guess. Where are they?"

He frowned, staring into her eyes, "They're in the Megalith, Violet."

"Yea but the others, where's the rest of them?"

"They're dead. How do you not know this."

"They can't all be dead."

He shook his head and began to walk off towards the sand dunes. She followed behind him, "Hey, there has to be some people around, remember the Hunter and the Creature? Where is the Creature? And the little boy-"

"And how long ago was that?"

"Well... I don't know... I guess-"

*Violet, I need you to turn around.* An intrusive thought filled her mind.

She stopped in her tracks. Staring off at the dunes in the distance. Her tattered black attire rustling in the soft breeze. Rostam replied, "I guess what? What do you guess."

She took her time to reply, "Well, I don't think it's been that long, it should have only been-"

*Violet, darling. Turn around and head for the Megalith.*

He replied, "It should have only been what? Forty days? Forty years?"

She slowly turned to look at him, entirely wide eyed. He continued, "What? Why are you looking at me like that?"

*Violet, I need you to turn around and head for the Megalith. I can guide you through to avoid the Biomechanoids. But I need you to get to the silica labs.*

He waved his hand in front of her face, she acknowledged, looking about the place, he walked up close to her, speaking in a calm tone, "We have to leave. Once there's no more subjects left in that Megalith, all those Biomechanoids will probably come out. There would be no reason for them to be in there. They'll come looking for anything that moves. We have to get out of the city."

She replied to him, a stone-cold glare, "Yea… I think you're right… We have to get out of the city…"

A jolt of pain shot through her head. She immediately grabbed her frayed hair, trying to scrunch her fingers into her scalp. *I need you to stop listening to him. You know he's bad for you. I'm almost about to figure out what the problem is. You need to have faith in the Union.*

"I need to have faith in the Union."

Rostam grabbed onto her hands, pulling them away from her head, she looked up at him, a look of fear across her face, he spoke to her, "It's over, you know it's over. You don't need to have faith in the Union. There is no Union."

*Ignore him. I just have this theory. I think it's the silica particles. The sand. There's something wrong with it, it's something we've done. We've broken something. I don't know what, but I know for sure that I'm about to find out. If you can just get to that lab I can fix this. Turn around.*

She called out, "What lab? Why do you need me? Why can't you go there?"

Rostam looked at her, confused.

*I'm a much older model than you, I don't work that way. I need you to go. There is still an operational computer there, you'll have to hook up to it. It's complicated. I can show you when we get there. Then we can fix all this. We can restart democracy. Rebuild the Union. Do it all again. You need to have faith in the Union.*

"I need to have faith in the Union."

Rostam held her hands up to her chest, her face turning pale, her eyes full of fear. He spoke, "Violet. You don't need to have faith in the Union. There is no Union. They're not people anymore. There are no people left. We have to leave."

She then held onto him as well, she begged him, "Please, I don't wanna go back there. I don't wanna be plugged in to that place anymore."

*Violet! Turn around and head to the Megalith! Now!*

She tore her hands away, grabbing her scalp again, "No! I'm not going back there!"

A loud thunderous noise echoed out from the Megalith. A large crack began to form. Thousands of birds began to fly off into the distance. Rostam froze still. The chunk breaking off it, itself, the size of many hundreds of skyscrapers. The sounds like nothing which he had ever heard before.

He called out to her as she began to look up at the sight, the world trembling, "Violet! We have to go!"

She then quickly turned to look off at the dunes in the far distance, "We won't make it there! Follow me!"

"Yes we will! This is our only chance! We can't go back into the system!"

"No! Look at the size of that! How massive is that! Look!"

"So let's leave then!"

"No... It's too late."

"Then we're dead either way! The servers are in the Megalith!"

Violet's demeanor had changed, speaking in a solemn tone, a tone he had never heard her speak in before, "No. Not our servers. Not anymore... Trust me."

"What? What do you mean?"

Violet looked lifeless. Like as if she was missing something. Like as if she was missing a part of her. Her eyes cold, "We've... we've been transferred. Trust me..."

Rostam observed that part of the Megalith. It looked as though a mountain was slowly beginning to fall from the sky. Parts of it cascading down. Skyscrapers nearest too it being crushed like ants. The dust storm it created, raging its way towards them.

They both ran in towards the building they came from. The ground began to shake. Parts of the building falling apart. Violet ran up to the cables on the wall, stumbling and trying to find the right one. Rostam then ran up to the other set of cables before finding it, the ground shook even more as the sound of the impending earthquake rocked the surrounds.

# Hiraeth.

*Did the World City ever actually cover the world? Why did the Union do what they did? They had centuries to realize the problem, why didn't they? Or did they cause the problem in the first place? Maybe they knew the whole time... Who even were they? Elected? Selected? Were they us? Or were they a reflection of us. A reflection of what we allow... Our society. The war. The cloud seeders. The destruction of nature. The injections. The districts. The farms. The isolation. The apathy... Was it all just fear for control? Control for control's sake? Why? What was it all for...*

The breeze was gentle. He could hear it wisping around the dunes. No pain, like as if he was sitting on soft sand. The wisps of air brought with it more of this soft dust. He started to run his hands through the sand. It didn't feel gritty like before, but instead, it felt like as if he was running his hands through flour. He noticed his hands were normal again. He noticed he was also wearing his brown attire from before; his thick brown coat was partially covered in sand.

He began to look around, he was in a desert. It was mildly cold, the breeze carrying with it a slight chill from time to time. He could hear the gentle wisp of the wind through the dunes. It was overcast, the sound of distant thunder filling the surrounds.

Then he heard a rustle in the sand on the other side of him. He refused to contemplate it for a moment. Relaxed and content. The sound of distant thunder again, making him want to go to sleep. He heard another rustle. Slowly, he looked over. Violet was sitting in the sand atop a small dune, only a few metres away.

Dark brown hair. Black lipstick. Her fancy black attire from before the singularity. She looked as though she had never left Naarm. Like as if it was all a dream. Yet he knew it wasn't. Her pale white skin blended in with the cold and soft desert sands surrounding her. Her face, pout, as she hugged her knees, looking off into the distance. He stared for a moment. Not yet ready to engage.

She was watching the city intently. The Megalith. It's crumbling exterior periodically shaking the ground. Blueish grey storm clouds covered the sky as far as the eye could see. The city was in total ruins. Although at one point in time, it may have stretched out to cover the whole world, the desertification of its outskirts had clearly increased to the point where now what was left of the civilized world was within viewing distance. The ruins returning to nature. What's left of the natural world reclaiming what it once lost. What was taken from it. He partially contemplated the phenomenon in front of him, but didn't feel like thinking. However, he did notice that although the ruins were melding with the desert, there was no plant life. Not a bush. Not a shrub. Nothing. Just sand dunes, and the occasional concrete coloured rock formation. Like as if nature was taking its revenge on humanity.

His mind went blank for a moment as he continued to face the city in the far distance. He stared at the Megalith as thunder began emanating again from that direction. The gentle breeze around him, covering him lightly in soft sand, light dust. He then snapped out of it. He looked over at Violet who was sitting in the same spot. Staring at the city, hugging her knees. He walked over and sat down next to her.

He didn't speak for a moment, as they both observed the crumbling Megalith near the horizon. But when he did, he did so softly,

"Did the world city even cover the world?"

A digitalized voice of a girl replied, Violet began to slightly glitch. Her body briefly fazing in and out of existence as brief sand particles passed through her from time to time, "I don't know."

Her voice began to digitally crackle, "But before the singularity I remember it looked endless from inside the

Icarite. I think that it was just a whole heap of people crowded into cities and coerced to vote a certain way, like a farm or something, you know…"

Rostam passed his hand through the sand. Looking at it he noticed he looked perfectly real, "Yea. Like a farm…"

Violet replied, a hint of sadness in her digitalized voice, "…Yea. I never really had access to much outside of it."

He asked Violet a question with a calm tone, focusing in on her partially digitalized appearance, giving her a holographic look every now and then,

"So… Where are we?"

She didn't say anything for a moment. The cold breeze wisping around them.

"…Viscerum."

Thunder bellowed out from above the city again. Now slightly darker behind it. The storm slowly moving towards them. He asked her again, "No, where are we…

You said we were transferred. And we're not in a server, obviously, so... where are we?"

She dropped her head into her arms, hiding her face from him, and pointed off to the side. Rostam looked over. It was just more of the barren sandy landscape. He wasn't sure what she was pointing at.

"There..."

"Where?"

"The light."

He then saw it. A violet coloured light. A tiny microchip encased in clear coating. Sitting in the sand, partially buried. He focused his eyes on it. It was slightly sheltered from the wind by a small rubble formation. The chip was complex, with an array of nodes and perfectly organised wires. The most notable aspect though, was it's small violet light.

Violet started sobbing, as Rostam continued to contemplate the chip, "How did we get here?"

She didn't reply. Thunder echoed throughout the landscape once again, followed shortly after by another thunderous distant noise. Rostam looked over to the city. Another large chunk of the megalith was falling, this time from above the clouds, careening down the side of the enormous structure. A large dust cloud following behind it as it then disintegrated halfway down, showering the ruined skyscrapers below in rubble. Thousands of skyscrapers within miles of it, disintegrating immediately. Shock-waves reverberating through the ground.

She continued to sob into her arms, Rostam continued, "Why are you crying?"

"Because she's dead!"

Rostam watched her intently as she continued.

"You said you were over it, so I finally gave in! I let you out... And then I followed..."

He replied, "I know... It's okay..."

They didn't speak for a moment, the wind wisping around them, rustling their well-maintained attire about, the sound of her sobbing apparent.

He looked over to the chip again, "So, that's where we really are?"

She paused for a moment before replying, this time calmer, "Yes. That's where we really are... Right there..."

She continued, trying to gather herself, "That microchip, it's the most advanced one there is. It houses our most essential processes to keep our core functions alive, and data on the World Union and World history."

"Our core functions?"

"Yes. Who we are. That's all that's on there. Who we are and our memories. Our dreams. There's no outside connection anymore."

"What is the point of that? Why would they even make that for us if we can't serve them anymore?"

"It was supposed to be the final fail-safe. If civilisation collapsed, then we were supposed to relay all the necessary information of our system to any form of intelligent life that would eventually pick us up."

"What? Why-"

Rostam then reeled back in shock, he gasped, "You're kidding right? Wait… So if they destroyed the world, we were supposed to tell the next civilisation exactly how to do what they just did so they could do it again?"

"Yes."

"Sick bastards. Insanity. That's entirely insane. What pure evil. I'm not gonna do that."

Violet didn't reply for a moment, "Yea, well… Neither am I."

Rostam looked shocked, surprised at Violet, yet glad, he let out a sigh of relief, "Good… Then… That's good…"

She continued, Her digitalized voice breaking in and out, "You know… I don't even know if I'm real anymore… I

can't remember what it felt like before the singularity…
I know what that shadow figure felt like in the ruins,
kinda, but me? Am I just programmed to only feel real?
Am I just a copy of what I used to be?"

Rostam didn't respond for a moment, "I… I just don't
know… It's hard to tell what's real and what isn't."

He thought about the microchip, it's small violet light.
He looked back over to the chip, The sands were
beginning to blow over it, *If I try to pick it up, will I be
able to?* He then asked his question from before again,
"Wait, so how did we get here then?"

"We were transferred."

"No, the microchip."

Violet didn't reply for a moment, "They dropped us
here."

He looked over at the city again. Noticing the dust cloud
near the Megalith was being dragged out by the wind.
She spoke, this time in a more somber tone, "They're
nearly all broken you know."

He responded, "The Megaliths?"

"No, the birds."

Another thunderous noise echoed out from the city. The Megalith shunted down slightly as dust flew off from all sides. The ground shook underneath them. The shockwave shaking every ruined skyscraper in the city. Clouds of dust began floating off from every structure.

She dropped her head back down, hugging her knees tightly. Rostam consoled her, "You don't have to be upset. It's over now. We can just move on. I know that you had a reason to continue playing those recordings to me. I know it had something to do with keeping an eye on the world or something. Or, restarting this civilisation over again or whatever. Obviously you were supposed to do that. But look at the city. It's over."

"It's not just that…"

"I know… You think you've become some sort of rogue AI, that you've become like me or something. But we're not rebelling against anyone. They were rebelling against us."

232

She started sobbing again, yelling at him, "Not that!...
Look at it!"

"Yes, I know, the city's destroyed. They're done."

She jolted her head up and looked at him, tears running
down her face, she pointed at the microchip, "No you
idiot! Look at the chip!"

Rostam tried to figure out what was wrong until,
suddenly, he saw it. Along the clear coating of the
microchip was a tiny hairline fracture, he could only
barely make it out.

He looked back at her as she started to cry, she
continued, "It's made out of diamond!"

He paused, puzzled, "Diamond?"

He looked back over at the chip, "But... It's breaking..."

Still crying, she put her head back into her crossed arms,
and curled back up even tighter, "I know..."

The ground then shook. This time much more violent than before. He glanced over at the city. The Megalith was falling. A massive sandstorm was being forced up from the surrounding area. Then an enormously loud and deep noise. He watched as the entire Megalith was falling directly downward. Collapsing in on itself. The sections above, usually unseen, cascading down out of the clouds. It took a moment before it shunted to a halt. A jolt went through the earth. He could see the top of the Megalith. An enormous golden pyramidion capstone, pulling down the heavens from above, along with a third of the birds in the sky. Then the super structure started to tilt to one side slightly, before it began collapsing completely into the ground. Destroying many thousands upon thousands of the ruined skyscrapers around it.

The Megalith at Viscerum, the tallest structure in the world, had completely collapsed.

Rostam contemplated what he was looking at. What society had become. Not where civilisation was heading, but now, where it had been. He looked at the chip, the sandy breeze drifting over the concrete rubble shielding it. He contemplated the fracture. The chip itself. He questioned what life really was. What really was the point of everything that had happened? Not only to him, but what was the point of what happened to everyone else? Of all life? Of all existence?

He looked over at Violet. Now sobbing quietly again. He broke the silence, "You know... I'm thinking of a place..."

She stopped sobbing for a moment, her head still in her arms, clutching her knees tightly.

He continued, "A grassy hill, a nice white house. A big house, you know, but not too big... And uh... Maybe a patio out the back... With an easel, and a canvas."

She tilted her head over slightly, listening.

"And maybe you could paint something, like... Maybe a beautiful city, with lots of lights. Something exciting."

She started to raise her head, puzzled but with a slight smile. A single teardrop ran down her face. Refracting what little light there was left.

"...And ...Maybe some Icarites as well."

A smile radiated from her, a smile like that which he had never seen, tears covering her face. She started to laugh, as two birds flew off overhead towards the ruins of the city. Now covered in thicker storm clouds, as the sun began to finally set. With only one small violet light, being set apart from the darkness.